YULETIDE PERILS

A Starstruck Novella

BRENDA HIATT

dolphin star
PRESS

Yuletide Perils

A Starstruck Novella

Copyright 2021 by Brenda Hiatt
Cover art by Fantasia Frog Designs

Dolphin Star Press

ISBN: 978-1-947205-29-1

Dedication

For my readers, who help to make the season bright!

If the Fates allow

M

I SETTLE into Rigel's arms with a happy sigh as the last slow dance begins, signaling the end of Jewel High's Winter Formal. I've had a wonderful time tonight with Rigel and the other four members of our newly-formed "Bond Squad"—a fitting reward after the harrowing events of last weekend. All six of us put our lives on the line, defying impossible odds by using our combined powers to avert a terrible disaster.

I'll say. How many times have we come crazy close to dying now? Rigel thinks to me, using the special telepathy our *graell* bond allows.

Individually? Or together?

His chuckle vibrates against my cheek, pressed to his chest. *Combined, at least half a dozen. I'd say we've earned a break,* he silently declares. *Hopefully a good, long one!*

I wholeheartedly agree.

As the music winds down, I take a last look around the paper-snowflake-festooned high school gym—an oasis of normalcy amid what too often feels like a scary sci-fi novel. Whatever happens after

I graduate high school in another year and a half, I'll miss moments like these.

Still, a thread of worry mars my contentment when my wandering gaze falls on my oldest friend, Brianna Morrison. She's partnered tonight by Liam Walsh, one of the newer *Echtran* students. A few feet away Debbi Andrews, my other best *Duchas* friend, is dancing with Liam's twin brother, Lucas.

Yesterday, when Bri and Deb told me about their dates, I barely hid my shock. I knew they'd asked Kira to drop hints to the Walsh boys, but I didn't think she really would. Or that the guys would follow through if she did. I wonder now if my friends would look as happy if they knew their dates recently moved here from Mars? Not that I, or anyone else, will tell them that.

Given that, I can't imagine either couple's relationships will progress much past a single dance date. Especially since Bri confided to me that Lucas had to be persuaded by Liam to ask Deb to the dance. Not surprising. Lucas strikes me as more level-headed than his brother, who tends to be rather impulsive. Like Bri.

On that thought, I glance over at the only other *Echtran-Duchas* pair in the room—Alan Dempsey and Trina Squires. Two weeks ago, I half-jokingly suggested Molly and Tristan nudge those two toward each other, to test their new bond-enhanced persuasive abilities. It obviously worked. But now, seeing Trina's besotted smile and Alan's slightly warier one, I realize that might not have been the best idea.

Looking back at Bri and Deb and their dates, my concern there mostly dissipates. They all seem happy tonight, and neither Walsh brother is the type to lead a girl on, knowing things can't really go anywhere. I trust even Liam to let Bri down easily, if necessary—unlike jerk-face Gary Chambers, who actually *admitted* he dumped her because she's biracial.

I just hope—

I break off that thought when I notice Rigel smiling down at me with a knowing look. I smile back.

That's better, he thinks to me. *I know you tend to borrow trouble, but don't do it tonight, okay? Especially about something as trivial as your friends' love lives, or lack thereof.*

You're right, I reply. *Anyway, winter break starts tomorrow, so I don't need to worry about things getting out of hand there for at least two weeks. Right now, I'd much rather focus on my own love life.*

I tilt my face up for a kiss and Rigel willingly obliges me, obliterating all other thoughts until he raises his head.

But then I regard him curiously. "You're keeping some kind of secret from me, aren't you? I thought I sensed it earlier, but now I'm sure."

He gives me a sheepish grin. "Sometimes I wish I were better at controlling my thoughts around you. Okay, yes, I am keeping a secret—but it's the good kind."

"Good kind?" I ask doubtfully.

"You *do* realize it's only a few days till Christmas, don't you?" Amusement sparkles in his gorgeous hazel eyes. "People are allowed to have a few secrets this time of year. You'll find out what it is next week."

I sense a trace of insecurity in those last words, so quickly assure him I'll love it, no matter what it is. "Though never as much as I love you," I add.

Rigel lowers his lips to mine and we finish out the dance with another wonderful kiss.

2

We won't go until we get some

Rigel

DIAMOND STREET IS MOBBED. I figured it would be, just two days before Christmas. Because Jewel, Indiana is known for its custom jewelry and artisan craft shops, people come here from all over the state to do last-minute shopping. But this is what I get for waiting so long to commission M's Christmas present from Glitterby's.

I hoped it would be ready sooner but they got so backed up, it was only this morning they called to say it's ready for me to pick up. So here I am in the middle of this mob scene, slowly making my way along the crowded sidewalk past Belinda's Books, Quilt World and the Jewel Art Gallery. As I go, I pick up *brath* from more than one *Echtran*—not surprising, since nearly two hundred of us live in Jewel now.

Even though there shouldn't be any dangerous *Echtrans* in Jewel now, I still glance at each one I sense, just in case. Though how I'd be able to tell, I don't know. It's only when M and I are touching that I can tap into her ability to sense emotions and intentions. By myself, all I can do is gauge expressions and make best guesses.

Maybe when M and I meet at Dream Cream in about twenty minutes, we should try a more thorough probe for anyone in town with evil on their mind. Just to be safe.

I finally reach Glitterby's, which is as packed as the street outside. I should have expected this, too, since their glass and crystal art and jewelry probably make great gifts. M ordered my Orion dreamcatcher from here for my birthday last year. Which is what inspired my idea for her Christmas present this year.

"Now, now, Gladys," old Agatha Payton, the proprietor, is saying to a woman at the counter as I come through the door. "Just one bag of beignets per purchase. And no, I can't sell you more, sorry. I'm not licensed to sell food here, so all I can do is offer my famous beignets as little extras—lagniappes, as they say in New Orleans—to boost business."

"Famous? Hah!" someone else in line for the register scoffs. "Only in your own mind, Agatha."

The shop owner glares at the scoffer, a woman who looks nearly as old as Agatha herself, despite her improbably bright red hair. "That's enough out of you, Ethel Ann," she snaps. "Every year you run down my beignets, but every year you want more than your share."

The redheaded woman just snorts and shakes her head, turning away to look at a purple glass statuette of an orchid on a nearby shelf.

"Everybody knows I make the best beignets in Indiana," Agatha continues, jutting out her chin. "Spent a whole year in New Orleans when I was a young thing, I did. Learned the trick from a handsome fellow who worked at the Café du Monde itself."

Several customers immediately pipe up to say how much they look forward to Agatha's beignets every year. "Why, it wouldn't be Christmas time without them," the woman at the register declares.

"Thank you, dearie." Agatha smiles. "Now, is this all you need today? I can giftwrap it if you want to come back."

"No, I'll wrap it myself at home, thanks. I need to be going."

Nodding, Agatha rolls the two glass vases in tissue and puts them in a bag. "Here you are, then. And your beignets, of course!"

She hands the woman a little bag of red cellophane, through which three things that look like powdered-sugar doughnut holes are visible. "Enjoy!"

The line's still long as I take my place at the end of it. I'm starting to worry I'll be late to meet M when old Agatha spots me.

"Hey there, Rigel!" she calls out. "That's right, everyone, I'm on a first name basis with Jewel High's star quarterback there. I've got your package right over here, all wrapped and ready." She points at a small collection of gaily wrapped boxes on a table near the register, each topped by a red cellophane bag tied with a green ribbon.

"Star or not, he can wait his turn to pay like the rest of us," the woman in front of me complains—the same red-haired one who scoffed before.

Agatha grimaces at her. "Ethel Ann, I've been telling you for twenty years that if you don't like the way I run my business, you're more than welcome to shop elsewhere. But anything to get you out of my store quicker. Here, you can be next, then I'll be free to enjoy the company of this handsome young man without your impertinence."

With a self-satisfied smile, Ethel Ann steps up to the cash register with an armful of glass knick-knacks. Once they're wrapped and rung up, she digs a credit card out of her purse.

"Your prices are highway robbery, you know that, Agatha," she comments sourly, shaking her head. "Nearly two hundred dollars for a bunch of stuff that'll probably break in shipping anyway." She snorts. "Now, where are my beignets?"

Agatha's eyebrows go up. "What, the ones you said are no good? I figured you wouldn't want any."

"They're at least edible," Ethel Ann allows. "Honestly, as much money as I spend here, I ought to get *two* bags. You at least owe me one."

"Guess you plan to *literally* eat your words, then, eh?" Agatha lets out a cackle. "But if that's what it'll take to get you out the door, fine."

Reaching over, Agatha plucks the cellophane bag off the top of M's little gift box, removes the sticker with my name, and hands it to the woman. "Serve you right if you choke on one." Then she leans over and whispers to me, "Those were getting a little stale anyway, Rigel. If you wait a minute, I'll have Janie get you some fresh ones from the back, still warm from the deep fryer."

"Um, okay. I've never had a beignet before, I don't think."

"Then you are in for a treat, young man," Agatha assures me, ringing up M's present. Handing me my receipt, she glances sharply toward the door. "Don't you dare open that bag in here, Ethel Ann!" she calls out. "You'll get powdered sugar all over my clean floor."

Ethel Ann smirks over her shoulder, then deliberately removes the ribbon from her cellophane bag. She makes an irritated little "tch!" sound as she reaches inside, then pulls out a pastry and pops it into her mouth. Powdered sugar goes everywhere, exactly like Agatha predicted.

"Why you insufferable, obnoxious—!" Agatha starts to exclaim, but breaks off when the other woman suddenly clutches at her chest.

Her bag of purchases falls to the floor with a tinkle of broken glass just before Ethel Ann collapses, right on top of it.

For an instant, the shop is silent. Then a babble of voices break out.

"Oh, Lordy, Agatha finally did her in!" "Must've been the beignet!" "Ethel Ann's always been a nasty piece of work but I never thought Agatha would actually kill her!"

A couple of people rush over to help the woman on the floor while others shout, "Somebody call 9-1-1!" and "Is anybody here a doctor?"

My mother is, but she's not here—and I unfortunately don't share her Healer ability. I'm pulling out my phone to call her when old Agatha grabs my arm.

Turning, I see her staring at her fallen foe, clearly aghast. "Is she… Is she…?"

A younger woman kneeling next to Ethel Ann puts an ear to her chest. "I don't hear a heartbeat. Does anyone know CPR?"

"I do, I'm a nurse," another woman says, hurrying forward.

"So do I," claims the only other male in the store.

The nurse begins chest compressions on the unconscious woman while Agatha tightens her grip on my arm. She's so pale, I'm afraid to move in case she falls down, too. In the distance, I hear sirens.

Looks like I'll be late meeting you, I send silently to M, since calling her right now would be awkward.

What's wrong? I hear sirens! Her thought is accompanied by alarm.

A customer just collapsed in Glitterby's. Someone called 9-1-1. Afraid they might be too late, though.

As the man takes over the chest compressions, a few accusing looks are directed Agatha's way.

"It wasn't me!" she protests, still gripping my arm. "I never liked Ethel Ann, but I'd never spoil my beignets by poisoning them! Think what that would do to my reputation!"

A moment later, a pair of EMTs come in, followed by Jewel's police chief and another officer—roughly half of Jewel's entire police force.

The EMTs move quickly to Ethel Ann's side, one continuing the CPR while the other opens a case containing defibrillator paddles and pulls up Ethel Ann's blouse. "Everyone back, please," he shouts out. "Clear!"

"Yes, why don't you all leave for now," a shaky Agatha echoes to those remaining in the shop. She's still clinging to my arm for support. "If you haven't paid yet, just set your things down and come back later. Let's give these men some space to work."

"No, everyone stay where you are," Chief Willis raps out, frowning around at the small crowd. "Until we can rule out foul play, you're all witnesses. Just stay put until we get statements from you."

As the EMTs repeatedly apply the paddles to the prone woman on the floor, I replay the last few minutes in my mind. The way Ethel Ann clutched her chest before falling, I assumed she had a sudden heart attack. Sure, the timing did look kind of suspicious, but nothing in that beignet could have affected her that quickly. She'd barely had time to swallow.

What kind of poison could possibly work *that* fast? None I know of. At least…none normally found on Earth.

"I'm so sorry, Rigel." Agatha makes a ghastly attempt at a smile as she finally loosens her grip on my arm. "I guess your fresh beignets will have to wait."

I nod mechanically.

"No, um, that's fine." I barely know what I'm saying. I'm too busy frantically, belatedly scanning the shop for any sign of Martian *brath*. I don't sense any, but I also don't know how many people left before Ethel Ann collapsed. Were any of them *Echtrans*? It now seems horribly likely.

Because if that beignet *was* what killed Ethel Ann, the poison in it must have been intended for me.

____

3

It's beginning to look a lot like...

____

M

ROUNDING the corner from Opal onto Diamond Street, I see two emergency vehicles with flashing lights in front of Glitterby's, two blocks away.

I quicken my pace. *Rigel?* I send in sudden panic. *Are you still okay?*

I'm fine.

The emotions I sense along with his reassurance tell me otherwise.

Are you trapped there or something?

After two long heartbeats during which I hurry another half block, he replies. *We all are for the moment. Chief Willis wants statements from everyone.*

I breathe a little easier. At least he's not being held hostage by yet another evil *Echtran* who wants him dead. That seems to be the first place my fears go these days. Not without cause, considering the number of threats he's faced over the past year.

A crowd, no doubt attracted by the sirens, lights and fast-spreading gossip, is gathered outside Glitterby's. With difficulty, I push my way through, catching snippets of whispered speculation.

"Sounds like old Agatha finally took care of Ethel Ann—permanently!" "To think, I've eaten her beignets for years and never—" "Agatha's always been a might testy, but I never thought she'd—"

I'm no longer able to pick up Rigel's thoughts, which spikes my worry again. At the curb, two men are loading an elderly red-haired woman into an ambulance on a stretcher. She looks vaguely familiar—either a Jewel resident or a frequent visitor.

When I'm finally able to peer into Glitterby's, I see Rigel speaking to Chief Willis. Relieved, I realize that's why he hasn't been sending any more thoughts my way. Reining in my impatience to get to his side, to touch him, I wait just outside the door until he's done.

"Hey," he whispers when he's finally allowed to join me out on the sidewalk. "We, um, need to talk. Dream Cream? Or the arboretum?"

My anxiety spikes again as I try to decipher the emotion I'm getting from him. "Arboretum," I decide. "We'll have more privacy there. Hot chocolate can wait. Can you start filling me in on the way?"

Throwing an arm around my shoulders, he gives a quick nod. *Don't want to say too much with all these people around, but...I think that woman might have been murdered. But not by Agatha Payton.*

I stare up at him, barely remembering to keep my feet moving forward. *Murdered? Really? I heard people whispering, but it sounded like pure speculation.*

It mostly was. The timing did make it look like Agatha had something to do with it, but—don't freak out, okay?—I think I was supposed to be the victim.

Now I do stop walking. We're well away from the throng around Glitterby's now, so I force Rigel to look at me. "What? Why?" I say aloud. "Are you sure?"

He shrugs. "Not sure, no. It's possible the woman just had a heart attack. But if not, if it really was poison... Well, the thing she bit into was supposed to have been mine."

"Huh?" I frown at him, confused. "How about you tell me *exactly* what happened."

Rigel glances up and down Diamond Street, still busy with shoppers. "Let's get to the arboretum first, okay?"

Despite my impatience, I agree. Two minutes later we go through the archway into the acre or so of walled garden that marks the end of the commercial section of downtown Jewel. Even with the flowerbeds dormant under a dusting of snow and the trees bare of leaves, the arboretum feels special—our special place.

Together, we walk to the green metal bench at the back where we've had so many crucial conversations in the past. I have a feeling this might be another one.

"Okay. Start with why you were in Glitterby's to begin with."

Rigel grimaces. "I wanted to keep this part secret, but…to pick up your present. I, uh, had them make something special for you."

"Aw!" I go up on my toes to kiss him on the cheek. "That's so sweet! But you don't have to tell me what it is. Just what happened after you got there."

With a nod and a crooked smile as we sit down on "our" bench, he continues. "Old Agatha Payton and this woman, Ethel Ann Something, were already snarking at each other when I walked in. I got the impression they do that regularly."

"Ah, it must have been Ethel Ann Riverton, then. I thought she looked familiar. According to Aunt Theresa, Ethel Ann and Agatha have been 'bosom enemies' since Aunt Theresa was a girl—so at least forty years. I've met her once or twice and she was pretty unpleasant—not that I'd have wished *this* on her, of course!"

"Me either," Rigel agrees. "Though like I said, it's possible she just had a badly timed heart attack."

I can tell he doesn't believe that. "So what happened next? Why do you think she might have been poisoned?"

"Agatha was giving away little bags of…beignets, I think she called them? With every purchase."

I nod. "She does that every year at the holidays. They're delicious."

"I wouldn't know." Rigel shrugs. "Anyway, this Ethel Ann made a crack dissing them, so Agatha didn't want to give her any. But then she made such a stink about it, Agatha gave her the bag that was sitting on top of the present I'd come to pick up—the bag that had my name on it. Agatha was just promising to get me some fresher ones from the back when Ethel Ann suddenly collapsed."

Now I'm confused again. "But...did she actually eat a beignet first?"

"Sort of. She opened the little crinkly bag, pulled out one of the doughnut things and stuck it in her mouth, then immediately grabbed her chest and fell down in a heap. I...I think she might have been dead before she even hit the floor. Pretty sure no regular Earth poison could have acted that fast. I don't think she even had time to swallow."

"Then...you think something *on* the beignet, or maybe inside the bag itself, is what killed her? Maybe the same toxin that killed Enid and that *Echtran* assassin before they could talk? Our Scientists up in Dun Cloch did say that whatever that stuff is, just a scratch from it can be instantly fatal. It's what almost killed Molly last month, too."

Rigel looks grim. "And you, last year. When that same guy attacked you right before Homecoming. Yeah. At least...it could have been."

"So if Ethel Ann hadn't interfered—" I break off in horror, imagining Rigel on that stretcher instead.

I start to shiver as it hits me how close I came to losing him. Again. Rigel puts a comforting arm around me, but that's not enough. Flinging my arms around his neck, I plaster my mouth over his, needing that extra reassurance that he's still here, still alive, still mine.

After a startled second, Rigel responds just as passionately. For a minute or two, all fear, mine and his, is swamped by our feelings for each other and the surge of strength and vitality kissing always gives us, thanks to our bond.

Eventually, the need to know more about what happened forces me to pull away, though I still lean into Rigel's warmth, beyond grateful for its continued presence.

"So, um, were there any other *Echtrans* in Glitterby's when this happened?" I ask, finding my voice again.

"Not that I noticed, but I didn't remember to scan for them until afterward. I *think* I'd have picked up on them anyway, but maybe not. I was in a hurry, wanting to get in and out so I could meet you at Dream Cream."

I grimace. "I didn't think to check for *brath* on my way to Glitterby's, either, I was so worried about you," I admit. "Maybe we should go back up Diamond Street now, see if we can find whoever did this? Their emotions would almost certainly give them away."

"You're right! I should have thought of that myself. Let's go."

On the way out of the arboretum, we pass a family of six coming into it. As crowded as downtown Jewel is today, we were lucky to have it to ourselves even briefly.

"I should call Kyna," I say as we hurry back toward the shopping district. "If there's a murderous *Echtran* in Jewel, the Council needs to know about it."

"Let's wait till we have some actual proof, okay?" Rigel suggests. "I mean, if it turns out Ethel Ann died of a simple heart attack, the Council might think I'm just paranoid."

"You have every right to be," I remind him. "How many times have you been targeted and nearly killed now? Three? Four? All by *Echtrans*."

He doesn't answer for several seconds. "Still… it doesn't look good if the Sovereign's Bodyguard seems more concerned for his own safety than yours. If the Council thinks I'm too easily scared, they could decide I'm not up to the job after all. Some of them never wanted me to have it in the first place."

"Then let me be the scared one," I tell him. "Do you have any idea what losing you would do to me? I'm not about to risk that for fear of what someone on the Council might think. If anyone suggests you're unfit, I'll point out that an attempt on your life just proves you're *so* effective as a Bodyguard, someone wants you eliminated."

We're nearly back to Glitterby's now, so we have to stop arguing, even mentally, to focus on the people around us. Walking slowly, hand in hand, we both stretch out with our senses to pick up any *brath* in the area. We do, almost immediately—but it's just Mr. and Mrs. Morain, Kira's parents, and there's nothing the least bit sinister about them. In fact, I clearly sense their genuine delight at seeing us.

"Ex— er, Miss Truitt!" Mrs. Morain exclaims, with a bob of her head that's fortunately well short of an actual bow. "How nice to see you again. You seem to be, ah, keeping well?"

"Very well, thank you." I manage a smile. "I hope you'll enjoy your first holiday season in Jewel."

They exchange a pleased glance, then beam at me. "I'm sure we will," Mr. Morain says. "Thank you!"

We continue to make our way toward Dream Cream, where our date was supposed to be, passing a few more *Echtrans* along the way. I carefully probe every person's emotions, even though I recognize most of them from NuAgra. The closest thing to a negative vibe I notice is one couple's slight disapproval, probably of Rigel, but it's nowhere near strong enough to suggest a recent murder attempt.

"Whoever it was, they must have bugged out of town when the cops showed up," Rigel says when we reach Dream Cream, opening the door for me. "That is, if someone really did…you know."

"I trust your instincts." *Especially since we don't know for sure that no bad guys live within an easy drive of Jewel*, I add silently as we move to an empty booth near the back of the little shop.

I sit down and Rigel goes to the counter for two hot chocolates. I'm tempted to try pushing my emotion-sensing power farther out, to take in all of Jewel, but I need Rigel's reinforcement for that—and Dream Cream isn't the best place for the kind of focus that would be necessary. Still, I can't help feeling like we're wasting time when a possible killer could be lurking.

"Are you *sure* you don't want me to tell the Council about this?" I ask when he returns with our steaming cups. "Whoever did this is likely to try again as soon as they find out they failed. Which they might have already."

Rigel frowns, clearly still conflicted. "Part of my job is to be prepared for any kind of threat. To you, mainly, but also to me or my family. Honestly, I'm more worried about the Council losing faith in me than another murder attempt. Let's at least wait till we're sure it wasn't just a heart attack."

"But...how *can* we be sure? If it was the same toxin that was used before, it more or less mimics a heart attack, so that's what the *Duchas* doctors will probably think it was. Even our own Healers were fooled at first."

He ponders that for a moment. "Maybe my mom can find out? Jewel's hospital isn't that big, and this was unusual enough that there'll probably be talk about it."

"It would look kind of odd for an OB/Gyn to ask to examine the body, wouldn't it? What about the bag that held the beignets? Maybe we should check that out instead," I say.

"Could be tough. The police secured it as evidence while they were questioning people."

Now my alarm spikes for a different reason.

"If it still has any of that toxin inside, anyone else who opens it could end up dead, too!" I quietly exclaim. "The last thing we need is multiple mysterious deaths when people are already suspicious of all these newcomers who've moved to Jewel."

I think for a moment. "Since you don't want to bring the Council into it yet, how about the rest of our Squad?" I suggest. "Maybe together we can come up with a way to get our hands on that bag before it can do any more harm."

"If so, we could also prove whether there really is an *Echtran* connection." Rigel agrees. "We need to do it soon, though. Someone else could examine that bag any time."

Nodding, I pull out my omni-phone. "Where should I tell them to meet us? Here is a little too public."

"The arboretum might be, too. I'd say my house, but my dad's probably home—and he's on the Council."

I try to think quickly. "Molly's mom is on the Council, too. And Tristan's. How about my house? If I even hint to Aunt Theresa that we'll be talking about, um, Martian stuff, she'll leave us alone, since it still kind of weirds her out. Plus, she's totally plugged into Jewel's gossip network. I'll be surprised if she hasn't already heard all the details of whatever the current story is."

He agrees to that, so I quickly message Molly, Tristan, Sean and Kira. They all agree to meet at my house in half an hour, so Rigel and I finish up our hot chocolates and head out.

———————————

4

Later on we'll conspire

———————————

Rigel

"I KNOW YOU WALKED HERE, but let's take my car." With some evil *Ecthran* possibly on the loose, I prefer keeping M close. There's no reason to assume I'm their only target.

She smiles up at me. "Sure. Especially since we have a little bit of extra time."

My heart speeds up at the suggestion in her voice. "I like the way you think," I murmur.

I had to park further up Diamond Street, the closest spot I could find with downtown so crowded. Though we keep checking for negative vibes along the way, M doesn't sense any—or any more *Echtrans*, either.

We walk quickly, increasingly impatient to make out some more. Stress seems to do that, to both of us. Finally pulling away from the curb, I drive to Opal Street, turn right, then pull over again before turning onto Garnet, M's street.

"You, ah, mentioned killing a bit of time?" I wink at her.

M responds by unfastening her seatbelt and leaning toward me.

18

For the next ten minutes, there's no room in my mind for worry. No room for anything but M, and how much I love her. Unlike last year, there are no longer any *official* impediments to our relationship, but we still don't get many opportunities to be truly alone. That makes us both eager to take full advantage of every brief chance we do get.

The feel of her lips on mine, the emotions zinging back and forth between us, restores my confidence that together, she and I can handle anything anyone throws at us.

Way sooner than I'd like, M straightens up with a little sigh.

"We should probably go, so the others don't get there ahead of us." I sense her reluctance, as strong as my own.

We'd both rather spend the next hour kissing.

"I'd better give Aunt Theresa a few minutes' warning, too," she adds, refastening her seatbelt even though her house is less than a block away. "She'll probably go into a dither worrying she doesn't have enough cookies on hand."

I chuckle at that. Mrs. Truitt takes justifiable pride in her cookie baking skills and never misses a chance to show them off.

A moment later I pull up in front of M's house and after one last, quick kiss, we both go inside. Mrs. Truitt is in the kitchen. Baking, as usual.

"Hi, Aunt Theresa," M greets her. "I've invited a few friends over to talk about some, um, semi-official stuff. Is it okay if we use the dining room table?"

Mrs. Truitt's eyebrows go up almost to her graying hairline. "Oh. Yes, yes, I suppose so. How many friends?" She shoots an anxious glance at her half-full cookie jar.

"Just four—Molly and Sean O'Gara and their steadies, Tristan and Kira. They probably won't stay more than an hour or so."

That prompts a look at the kitchen clock, probably to reassure herself that we'll all be gone well before dinnertime. "That will be fine. I'll put something together for you all to nibble on," M's aunt says with a nervous smile.

Now that she knows the truth about who M really is, Mrs. Truitt acts a lot more respectfully toward her. A welcome change, in my opinion. When she thought M was just some random orphan she'd inherited from her husband's relatives, she practically treated her like an unpaid servant.

After M sets water for tea on the stove to boil, she and I carry six cups into the dining room, along with sugar and a little pitcher of milk. By the time the doorbell rings, the tea is brewing in a big, flowered teapot. M sets it on the table and hurries to let everyone in.

"Hey guys, what's up?" Molly asks as she and Tristan follow us into the dining room, Sean and Kira right behind them. "M's message was a little cryptic."

"I figured it would take too long to explain in a text," M tells her. "But something happened in downtown Jewel a little while ago I think we should discuss."

As soon as we're all sitting down, Mrs. Truitt comes in with a heaping plate of Christmas cookies. She only stays long enough to greet the four newcomers before scurrying back to the kitchen. Guess M was right.

While the others help themselves to tea and cookies, M and I describe today's incident at Glitterby's and why I believe it could have been an attempted murder—of me.

"But you don't actually *know* that, right?" Sean asks, his coppery brows drawn down in a frown.

"No," I admit. "Which is why I didn't want to bring the Council into it yet. M and I were hoping if we all put our heads together, we might come up with a way to prove it. Or disprove it, if I'm wrong."

Molly looks thoughtful. "Do the police believe Agatha poisoned the woman?"

"They definitely didn't come out and say so," I reply. "Not while I was there, anyway. I left before they were done questioning all the witnesses. I'm sure she didn't, though. I was standing right next to Agatha when it happened and she was as shocked as everyone else."

"Agatha's probably not in any real danger of being charged with murder," M says. "Even if Ethel Ann was poisoned, it'll probably be ruled a heart attack, at least if it was the same *Echtran* toxin that assassin tried to use on Molly. That's more or less how it works, according to the Healers in Dun Cloch."

Sean's still frowning. "It sounds like that bag of whatevers is the key to proving it one way or the other."

"That was our thought, too," I say. "Plus if I'm right, and the woman died from just touching something inside that bag, we need to get to it before anyone else messes with it."

"Exactly," M says. "Like I told Rigel earlier, we definitely don't need a string of suspicious *Duchas* deaths in town—especially at the holidays. Besides, the sooner we know whether someone tried to kill Rigel, the sooner we can start planning how to take them out of commission."

Everyone murmurs their agreement with that.

"If the cops took the cookie bag with them, they probably put it in some kind of evidence room," Tristan says. "At least, that's what they do on NCIS and all those type shows. I don't suppose any of you know where that would be, exactly?"

M shrugs. "Jewel's police station is a kind of annex attached to the City Hall. It's not very big—I was inside once on a field trip in sixth grade. One holding cell, a couple of offices and a main reception area, that's all I remember. Any 'evidence room'—" She makes air quotes— "is probably just a little closet or something. I'm sure they'd keep it locked, though."

Kira speaks up for the first time. "I wonder if Sean's and my new ability could unlock a door? Or at least get hold of the key without anyone noticing?"

"First we'd need some reason to visit the police station," Sean points out. "Can anyone think of one?"

"Maybe one of us could say our dog has gone missing?" Molly suggests. "Do the cops deal with that kind of thing?"

Tristan shrugs. "No clue. Maybe we could pretend we want a tour, say it's for a school project?"

"Probably more believable," M admits. "Especially since half the town knows we've never had a dog."

"We do," Kira volunteers, "but I doubt my sister's willing to lose her for the cause. They're pretty attached."

I think for a moment. "What if we claim we saw something suspicious nearby? Like someone breaking into the church? That might get some of them to go outside, give us a chance to—"

"Get caught messing with the evidence room?" Sean interrupts, one eyebrow raised. He looks at Molly. "Maybe you and Tristan can do your thing and schmooze our way in? Or at least find out what their holiday schedule will be like, see if there'll be a chance to sneak in when hardly anyone will be there."

Molly and Tristan exchange a glance. "I guess we could try," she says. "We still need a reason to go there in the first place, though."

We kick around a few more possibilities, some fairly outlandish, then M speaks up.

"I have an idea," she says. "Why don't Molly and I go to the station tomorrow morning? I'm on the school newspaper staff, so I can claim I'm writing an article about Jewel's various government offices, including theirs. Once school starts back up, I could even pitch it to Angela. While we're there, Molly can use her persuade-y thing to find out their holiday schedule and where they keep evidence. Then we can go from there."

Everyone agrees that's the best plan yet. With that decided, we all leave a few minutes later.

M walks me out to my car. "I'll let you know if I hear anything," she tells me. "I'll be surprised if what happened at Glitterby's isn't the main topic at dinner tonight. Uncle Louie's sure to hear about it at work, and if Aunt Theresa hasn't already, I imagine she will soon. If anyone else *has* died, that news is bound to be circulating already, too. Meanwhile, be really, *really* careful, okay?"

The distress in her green eyes compels me to kiss her fears away, as best I can in such a public setting.

"I will. I promise," I murmur against her lips. "You be careful, too. Until we know exactly what we're dealing with, we should all be on our guard. But try not to worry too much, okay? Who knows? Maybe Ethel Ann really did just have a heart attack and we're freaking out over nothing."

I can tell M doesn't believe that any more than I do.

5

Is gonna spy

M

I PRETEND to be reassured by Rigel's words until he drives away, even though I can tell he doesn't believe this will turn out to be "nothing" any more than I do. He only said that for my sake—but we're way too closely bonded now to hide our true feelings from each other. That gets a little inconvenient sometimes, but I wouldn't have it any other way.

After a moment, I go back inside to help Aunt Theresa with dinner. I'm in the middle of mashing the potatoes when the corded phone on the kitchen wall rings.

My aunt hastily dries her hands to pick up the receiver. "Hello? Oh, no, I hadn't!" I hear excited chattering on the other end and make a pretty good guess what about. Finally, Aunt Theresa makes a few noncommittal noises and hangs up.

"That was Louise Batten," she tells me. "She says there was a death, possibly a *murder* at Glitterby's today! You were downtown earlier, weren't you? Did you hear anything about it?"

"I, uh, may have heard some gossip, but I didn't pay much attention. I was meeting Rigel at Dream Cream." That last bit's true, at least. "What did Ms. Batten say happened?"

Before she can answer, Uncle Louie comes in through the kitchen door, his eyes bright with excitement. "Did you hear? Word's going around that old Agatha Payton finally got rid of Ethel Ann Riverton —permanently!"

"Louise just told me the same thing," Aunt Theresa tells him. "Something about a poisoned beignet?"

"Did the police actually arrest Agatha?" I ask in sudden concern.

To my relief, Uncle Louie shakes his head. "Not yet. Just took her in for questioning…so far. That's what Tom told me, anyway. His wife was downtown when it happened and she said witnesses sounded pretty split on whether it was poison or a heart attack. Guess we won't know for sure until they do an autopsy."

As I predicted, the topic dominates our dinner conversation, though I don't let on that Rigel was an eyewitness. No one seems to have heard about any other deaths so far, thank goodness. If Chief Willis had already opened that bag and dropped dead, I'm sure the news would be all over town by now.

Before going to bed that night, I call Molly to fine-tune our plan for tomorrow morning. Then, just before falling asleep, I mentally touch base with Rigel. We do this every night—one of the nicest things about our bond.

Let me know how things go at the police station tomorrow, as soon as you finish, he sends sleepily.

I will. I love you, Rigel.

My fears temporarily lulled by his warm response, I snuggle under the covers and drift off to sleep.

Molly stops by shortly after breakfast the next morning, ostensibly so we can go downtown for some last-minute Christmas shopping.

"Most of the stores will be closing early today," Aunt Theresa cautions us as I get my coat. "I assume you'll both be at the Cantata tonight?"

"Of course." We certainly plan to be. Our church's Christmas Eve Candlelight Cantata is an annual tradition. Both Aunt Theresa and Mrs. O'Gara are in the choir, so it would look odd if we weren't there.

A few minutes later, Molly and I head out—on foot, since neither of us has a car. Jewel's City Hall is at the opposite end of Diamond Street from the shops, just a block from our church on Ruby Street, but we don't turn that way until we're out of sight from my house in case my aunt is watching. As always, our adult Bodyguards, Cormac and Gilda, shadow us from half a block back, but discretion is part of their job description.

"You realize," Molly says as we walk, "our whole plan will be pointless if they've already sent that bag of beignets off to some lab for analysis."

I nod. "Rigel already mentioned that. But it's pretty much all we have—and maybe we'll get lucky."

"Unlike poor Mrs. Riverton." Molly shakes her head sadly. "If Rigel's right and that toxin was intended for him, she just got caught in the crossfire."

"Yeah. That wasn't fair at all, even if nobody much liked Ethel Ann. She made my Aunt Theresa seem like a complete sweetheart by comparison. Still, she didn't deserve this. I doubt even Agatha Payton would have wished it on her, much as they always detested each other. I just hope no one else will suffer her fate—assuming they haven't already. "

When we reach the police station a few minutes later, I'm startled to see it looks closed. There's a sign on the door that reads: *For Emergencies, please call 911 or the number below to be forwarded to the officer on call. Merry Christmas!*

Molly and I exchange a disbelieving look. Surely it can't be *this* easy? Then I notice movement inside and realize a woman is sitting at the main desk. I try the door handle and it's unlocked.

The woman looks up with a smile as we enter. "Oh, hello, dears, merry Christmas. What can I do for you? There's been no more trouble, I hope?"

"You mean what happened yesterday, at Glitterby's?" I ask.

"There's been nothing else we know of, but we were hoping to find out more about that incident. We're on the school newspaper staff and we both plan to become real news reporters after high school. We'd very much like to write an article about it."

That exhausts my rehearsed speech. The woman frowns like she's about to refuse and send us on our way, but then Molly speaks up.

"There aren't many opportunities to break important stories in a town as small as Jewel," she explains. "It would really help us out a lot if you could tell us what you know about it."

I can tell she's using not only her Royal "push" but that extra persuasive ability she has. It's become a lot stronger since she and Tristan bonded, probably because he already had a somewhat similar talent. When the two of them combine forces, they're almost irresistible.

The woman's frown disappears and for a second her eyes lose focus. Then she nods, her smile back in place. "Of course, dears. I'm happy to help a pair of budding young reporters. What do you need to know?"

"We understand a woman collapsed in Glitterby's yesterday with what appeared to be a heart attack, but there are rumors circulating that it could have been something else. Is Agatha Payton under suspicion for anything to do with it?" I use some "push" of my own as I ask.

Slowly, the woman nods again. "She hasn't been arrested, but Chief Willis had her come in for questioning yesterday afternoon. She swore up and down she had absolutely nothing to do with Ms. Riverton's demise, though from what I overheard, the timing was rather suspicious."

"Suspicious?" Molly echoes. "Why?"

"According to witnesses, Ms. Riverton had just taken a bite of one of Ms. Payton's Christmas beignets before she collapsed. Unfortunately, most everyone in town knows how much those two women always hated each other. The fact that Ms. Payton made the beignet herself and gave it to Ms. Riverton with her own hands also seems rather incriminating. I suppose we won't know for sure until the county lab in Anderson can analyze what's left of that beignet."

I suck in a breath. "Has it already been sent there? How long do they usually take with that sort of thing?"

"With the holidays, who knows?" The woman shrugs. "They're closed today and tomorrow, so we're keeping it here until someone can run it over the day after Christmas." She glances over her shoulder. "But there's no big rush, I suppose. It's not like the results will bring poor Ms. Riverton back, rest her soul. Of course, Agatha Payton's been told not to leave town."

"I, ah, assume you keep evidence like that somewhere fairly secure?" Molly asks, pen poised over the pad of paper she brought along.

"Oh, yes!" the woman replies, clearly still under Molly's influence. "We don't have a proper evidence room like some bigger departments, but the cabinet we use for such things is always locked. Can't imagine anyone other than Agatha Payton would want to steal it, and that would only be if it really is poisoned. If she's telling the truth, she'll want the lab to confirm it's not."

Relieved, I cautiously let out my breath. "Then…no one has handled it since it was brought in?"

"No, I believe it's still in the evidence bag Chief Willis put it in at Glitterby's."

I glance at Molly, who gives me a tiny nod.

"I'm glad to hear you're keeping the evidence safe for now," she tells the woman. "Would you be willing to double check on it? I'd love to report on how impressive your security here is."

The woman blinks twice, then stands up. "I suppose that's a good idea. We do take our security quite seriously, as you might imagine." Reaching up, she plucks a key off one of several hooks on the wall above her head. "I believe it's this one."

Turning to a tall, metal cabinet, she unlocks it and turns the handle, opening the door. "Yes, see? There it is on that shelf, still in the evidence bag, like I said. There's been absolutely no tampering on my watch, you can tell your readers that."

"We certainly will," I assure her.

She's just relocking the cabinet when a uniformed officer comes out of one of the rooms at the back of the station.

I freeze, sure he's going to ask why she opened the evidence cabinet, but he just says, "I'm taking an early lunch, Cathy, need to do a bit of shopping for the missus before the stores close. Tell the Chief if he comes back before I do, okay?"

"Of course, Daniel. Good luck with your shopping." She replaces the key on its hook and turns back to us. "Was there anything else you girls would like to know?"

"I, ah, don't believe so," Molly replies. I can sense her relief, as strong as my own. "But will it be all right if we come back sometime this afternoon if we think of more questions?"

"Not too late," the woman cautions us. "We'll all be going home at four today, what with it being Christmas Eve and all. Closed tomorrow, too, though of course two officers will always be on call for emergencies. Hope we don't have any, so they can enjoy the holiday with their families. That's as it should be, don't you think?"

Molly and I heartily agree.

"Thank you so much, Ms...Fernwood." I glance at the nameplate sitting on the desk. "You've been a great help. If our article is good enough, maybe they'll even run it in the Jewel Daily Gem." Rarely more than eight pages, mostly ads, it's the closest thing Jewel has to a local newspaper.

With a final exchange of cheery Merry Christmases, Molly and I leave.

"Wow, that really was easier than I expected," I say when we're half a block away from the station.

"No kidding. And well done, you, setting it up so I could ask her to confirm about the evidence bag. Now we know exactly where it is, and the key, too! Let's tell the others right away."

She pulls out her phone—an omni-phone similar to mine that she's only had for a few weeks. While she's calling Tristan, I mentally reach out to Rigel.

We just left the police station. The bag is still there and tonight will definitely be our best chance to get it.

Only a few seconds pass before he responds, *Good job! Your reporter story worked, then?*

Along with Molly being Molly. I go on to describe our encounter with the woman at the desk, including the close call just before we left. *We should all meet up ASAP to come up with a plan to get that bag.*

He agrees, so I look to Molly, who's still talking to Tristan.

"When can he meet us?"

"Anytime," she says. "Right away, if the others can make it."

I relay that to Rigel, who suggests the arboretum as the most private location we're likely to find on Christmas Eve. I pass that on to Molly, who tells Tristan, who says he'll message Sean and Kira.

"Your way is so much quicker," she says, putting away her phone. "I hope Tristan and I develop that much range eventually. Anyway, we should get walking. They could all get there ahead of us, since we're at the opposite end of town and on foot."

We pick up our pace and reach the arboretum ten minutes later, only slightly out of breath. Sean and Kira are already waiting at the entrance and Tristan's car arrives as we join them. Just behind him, Rigel also pulls into the little lot.

"Is the arboretum empty?" he asks as he and Tristan walk over to us.

I do a quick emotion-scan of the interior to check. "Yep, seems to be. Come on."

We go far enough in to be out of sight from the entrance, then face each other in a rough circle.

"So," I begin. "Molly and I found out the police station will be completely deserted tonight. Officers will be on call, but that's it. The trick will be breaking in without anyone noticing and calling them. Any ideas?"

"Too bad invisibility isn't anybody's superpower," Tristan quips. "That would be super convenient right now."

Everyone laughs at that.

"Our best bet is to wait till late," Rigel says, "when no one will be around. But that'll mean sneaking out of our houses without making any of our parents suspicious."

We all ponder that new difficulty until Molly exclaims, "No! It won't! Tonight's the Candlelight Christmas Eve Cantata at church, remember? Our mum, M's aunt and Kira's mum are all in the choir."

"So's mine," Tristan adds, grinning again. "She joined it just last week."

"Perfect! So they'll all be there anyway—assuming your parents plan to come?" I ask Rigel, who nods.

"The concert is supposed to start at nine, right?" Sean says. "If we can somehow slip out right as it starts, we'd have nearly an hour before anyone's likely to start looking for us."

I think back to years past. "If we all get there a little late, we'll probably have to sit in the back, since it's usually pretty crowded," I tell the others. "That would make it easier."

Molly nods excitedly. "I have it! We can claim there's some school-related Christmas Eve party earlier, so we'll meet our parents there. But…assuming we do get away unnoticed, how do we get into the police station? Anybody have lock-picking skills?"

My optimism falters as we all shake our heads.

"Tell you what, though, I can study up on it today," Rigel offers. "I'm sure there are online tutorials. Before I go home, I'll swing by the station, take a look at what kind of lock they have. First, though, I should go back to Glitterby's. If they're still giving out beignets, I can get another bag to swap out for the one we'll take."

I smile up at him. "You're better at this sort of thing than I realized. Okay, assuming we can somehow get in, let's figure out what to do once we're inside. I'd rather we not have to do too much improvising on the fly."

Privately, though, I suspect that will be inevitable.

6

Not a creature was stirring

Rigel

OUR GROUP SPENDS another half hour strategizing various contingencies for tonight before Sean and Kira have to go meet Kira's parents for lunch.

"Molly and I need to buy something somewhere to justify our so-called shopping trip," M tells me as we all leave the arboretum.

"We'll come with you," Tristan says. "With a possible killer on the loose, you two shouldn't be wandering around without Bodyguards."

I fully agree. Though I'm sure their Council-appointed adult Bodyguards are lurking somewhere nearby, I always feel better when I'm right next to M myself—for all kinds of reasons.

Leaving our cars in the arboretum lot, Tristan and I accompany our girlfriends up Diamond Street. I do my best to push aside thoughts of everything that could go wrong tonight so I can simply enjoy the feel of M's hand in mine. Any chance to spend time with her is good, even on a public, bustling street. Also, I can't worry too much without her picking up on it and worrying, too.

"Why don't I stop in at Glitterby's now?" I say as we approach the shop. "Maybe I can learn a little more, too."

We all go in. The store isn't nearly as crowded as yesterday—just two or three other people browsing. Because it's Christmas Eve? Or because of what happened to Ethel Ann?

I get my answer when Agatha spots me and hurries over.

"Ah, Rigel! Have you come back for your beignets?" Worry lines around her eyes add to her usual wrinkles. "Most haven't. Even people buying things today mostly aren't taking them. Guess word got around." She casts a sad glance at a whole pile of red cellophane bags near the register.

"Er, yeah," I tell her. "Several people have told me how good they are. The police don't really think you poisoned that woman, do they?"

Agatha snorts. "Guess there's no knowing what they think. But ain't nothing wrong with my beignets, never has been!"

She says those last words loudly enough for everyone in the shop to hear, prompting a few nervous looks.

"I'm more worried what all my regular customers think," she confides in a lower tone. "This could ruin my business—even once their tests prove I didn't poison anybody. Which they will! Probably won't stop the gossip, though, knowing this town."

We all make sympathetic noises, agreeing that's not fair, which gets a smile from Agatha. Grabbing up several bags of beignets, she hands them around to us.

"Here, take a couple bags each. Might as well. I made 'em all fresh this morning and they're no good stale. I'll never eat all these myself." She shakes her head sorrowfully at the remaining pile. "Now, is there anything else I can get you? Any of you?"

M and Molly each buy a little glass figurine, which clearly pleases Agatha.

"Thank you so much, Ms. Payton," M says as Agatha wraps up their purchases. "I'm sure business will bounce back once the police hear from the lab that those beignets were fine."

The old woman shrugs. "Time'll tell. I'm just lucky it didn't happen till the tag end of the Christmas rush—no thanks to Ethel

Ann. Not saying she *planned* to drop dead in my store, but if anyone would have, it would've been her. God rest her soul and all that."

A moment later we're all back out on the sidewalk with our bags of beignets, heading back to the arboretum and Tristan's and my cars.

"Poor Agatha," M sighs as we walk. "She's probably right that it'll take a while for the gossip to die down even after she's proved innocent. This town!" She shakes her head.

Even though the girls only live a few blocks away, Tristan and I drive them home. We *are* their Bodyguards, after all. And why miss a chance to make out?

After ten minutes of glorious kissing, I'm in a great mood when I drop M off, despite the likelihood that someone wants to kill me.

As planned, I swing past the police station on my way home. Stopping on Onyx Street almost, but not quite, across from the entrance, I wait till I'm sure no one's watching and snap a few high-def pictures of the lock with my omni-phone to analyze later. From here, it appears to be one of those new electronic ones, which is cool. With any luck, M and I can use our electrical ability to short it out.

The security camera above the door is another issue—especially if there are more inside. I take a couple pix of that, too, then pull away from the curb before anyone notices me here and gets suspicious.

As I continue home, I try to think of anything else, apart from that camera, that we haven't accounted for. If we've missed anything important, tonight's caper could easily turn into a disaster. Determined to prevent that if at all possible, I spend the whole afternoon online, researching security systems and how to circumvent them.

My dad would be a great resource, but I can't very well ask him without letting him know why I need to know—which he'd have to pass along to the Council. Until I know for sure my suspicion is justified, I'm not willing to do that.

It's true I don't want the Council to think I'm too easily spooked, but not just because that wouldn't be fitting for a Bodyguard. Already, the Royals on the Council—along with a sizable percentage of our people—consider me totally unworthy of the Sovereign's affections. I refuse to give them one more reason to believe that.

"Wow, I've never seen this place so crowded," I comment as I join M and the others near the back of the sanctuary at two minutes past nine that evening.

M chuckles. "It's like this every year. The regulars always come, along with all the folks who only show up at church on Christmas Eve and Easter. That *should* make it easier for us to sneak out without being noticed."

Sure enough, all the pews appear to be packed. I see my parents two-thirds of the way up, sitting with Kira's dad and Mr. O'Gara, but there are no spaces near them. My mom glances back and I smile and shrug, pointing at the row of chairs along the back wall for latecomers. She nods, then leans over to tell the others, who also turn to look at us.

"Good, our folks know we're here," Sean says. "Once things start, I doubt they'll turn around again till the service is over."

Our group snags the six chairs nearest the door—and wait. I can sense M is as impatient as I am. The others probably are, too. Finally, the choir files in and a hush falls over the sanctuary. A moment later, ushers start moving down the center aisle, passing out little white candles with cardboard guards to protect hands from hot wax. The pastor goes to the altar and begins reading the Christmas story from Luke.

By the time he finishes, everyone has a candle—even us. Now the ushers head down the center aisle again, this time with long-handled lighters, lighting the first candle at each pew, so the flame can be passed along the row. They're halfway to us when the choir starts singing.

"I think this is our cue," I whisper to the others. They nod and we all half-stand to quickly make our way out the door at the back of the sanctuary.

Once outside, we wait a moment, tensely listening.

"Do you think anyone noticed us leaving?" Molly asks anxiously. "If Mum—"

"She wasn't watching. I looked," Sean assures her. "Even if she does realize we're gone, she can't do anything about it until the end of the service. With any luck, we'll be back by then. I trust you to come up with a good excuse if we need one."

Everyone chuckles. Molly's ability to improvise when needed is legendary—among us, anyway.

Keeping a wary eye out for anyone who might notice us, we head up Emerald to the Jewel City Hall, which takes up the whole block between Ruby and Diamond Streets. The police station is off to the right, its separate entrance facing Onyx Street.

The three of us with Bodyguard training carefully scan the area, but all appears deserted at the moment. Not surprising, really. Other than special events like tonight's Cantata, the only things open this late in downtown Jewel are Green's Pub and the Lighthouse Cafe, further down Diamond. Even those are likely closed on Christmas Eve.

I put up one hand to make everyone halt, then point with the other. "See that security camera mounted above the door? We need to take care of that before we get too close. I'm hoping Sean and Kira can help there."

Pulling the pad of sticky notes I swiped from Dad's desk drawer out of my pocket, I peel off the top one and set it on my palm, sticky side up. "Think you guys can maybe float this up there and stick it to the lens?"

Though clearly surprised, Sean and Kira exchange a brief look, then focus on the little piece of paper I'm holding. Barely a second passes before it rises off my palm and drifts down the street toward the station. I hold my breath as they maneuver it into position just above the camera, then lower it over the lens.

"Now we need to apply enough pressure for it to stick," Sean mutters to Kira. "Not too much—we don't want to break it. Careful, careful... Okay, let go."

We all keep watching for a long moment, but the sticky note stays put.

"Great," I say. "Good thing it's not too windy tonight. Let's move."

All six of us hurry the rest of the way to the station, then up the four concrete steps to the door.

Tristan eyes the complicated-looking lock with its keypad. "Now what? Did you figure out how to get in?"

"I think so. Just a sec." I take out my phone and pull up what I found online about this lock's make and model. "It's a double-secured lock, which means even if we knew the combination—which we don't—a registered user would have to confirm it from an alert they'd get on their phone. So we obviously have to bypass that."

I click to the page on the company's website I bookmarked earlier, the one that's only supposed to be accessible to installers. Fortunately, I'm way more adept at getting past password protections than I used to be, after hacking into a bunch of conspiracy groups a few weeks back.

"The manufacturer's master code should get us in, but first we need to knock out the wifi signal, to keep it from sending anyone an alert. Pretty sure doing that will also disrupt the security camera's feed. That way, even if anyone notices something later, they'll hopefully assume it was just an internet glitch. Look inside. Do you see anything that looks like an internet router?"

Sean peers through the thick glass of the door. "There's a vertical row of lights on a shelf behind the front desk. That's probably it. Can you and M zap it from here?"

M grins. "Considering we generated eight gigajoules of electricity to stop the Grentl, we should be able to manage the teensy amount this will take."

"Can you let us do it?" Tristan asks eagerly. "Molly and I haven't had a chance to use our electrical thingy since those tests you did."

I shake my head. "Better not. It'll be tricky to generate just enough electricity to force a reboot without permanently frying the router, and M and I have the most practice." I turn to her. "Ready?"

Nodding, she steps to my side and squints through the glass. "I see it." She grabs my hand. "On three?"

"On three. Lowest possible setting. Oh, wait. Somebody see if you can find the station's network on your phone. It'll be locked, but the name might make it obvious."

"Got it," Molly says a second later. "At least, I assume 'JPD Official Private' is it. There's also a locked 'JPD Guest' signal. Both probably from that router."

I tell Molly to let us know when the wi-fi signal disappears, then glance at M. *Think about going negative, for a stasis field, then just a tiny bit positive from there.* She nods. "Okay," I say aloud, for the sake of the others. "One, two, three!"

Together, we aim the smallest possible electrical charge at the router behind the desk. Then wait.

"Signal's still there," Molly reports after nearly a minute passes.

By now, I'm starting to get nervous someone will drive past and wonder what we're up to.

"This glass is really thick," M comments. "Maybe we need to compensate for that?"

"Good point," I say. "Let's kick it up half a notch."

We try again and a second later Molly reports that both JPD signals are gone. Immediately, I punch the master code into the lock's keypad. It buzzes open and we all scoot inside, shutting the door behind us. We're all wearing gloves, cold as it is, so no worries about leaving fingerprints.

A quick glance at the router behind the desk shows it dark, but then all the lights on it start flashing.

"We need to swap out the bags and get out before it finishes rebooting," I mutter over my shoulder.

Molly quickly nips behind the desk and plucks a key off the wall above her head. "This is the one she used, right, M?" Not even waiting for M's nod, she fits it into the handle of metal cabinet next to the router and opens it.

There, on the top of three shelves, sits the evidence bag I recognize from Glitterby's yesterday. Molly reaches in and grabs it, then sets it on the desk.

"It's sealed," Kira says, leaning in close to look. "Will we be able to reseal it so they won't know we opened it?"

Sean steps forward. "The heat setting on my omni should do it. Want us to try using our powers to unseal it without touching it?"

"No time," I say. Already one of the lights on the router has stopped flashing.

I peel up the sticker across the evidence bag's flap and pull it open. Inside is a red cellophane bag just like the one I brought along.

"Careful!" M cautions. "The bag itself might be poisoned."

"Let us do this part, then," Sean suggests.

This time I nod.

He and Kira concentrate and the cellophane bag floats out of the evidence pouch and onto the desk beside it. "Now what?" Sean asks.

I pull out the plastic zipper bag I brought along, turn it inside out, and pick up the Glitterby's bag. Two and a half beignets are visible through the translucent cellophane. Setting down the purloined bag, I take out the newer one I brought with me. Opening it, I take a bite out of one beignet, then put it back in the bag. "Close enough?"

No one objects, so I stick the new bag into the evidence pouch and motion to Sean, who uses his omni to reseal it with the sticker I peeled off. Molly puts the evidence bag back into the cabinet and locks it, then replaces the key.

M hastily brushes powdered sugar off the desk. "I doubt they'll notice anything unless they have a reason to be suspicious," she says, examining the surrounding area for any she missed.

"Hope not," I say. "No time to worry about it now—router's nearly back online." Only one light is still flashing. "Let's get out of here."

Tristan pushes open the door and sticks his head out to look up and down the street. "Coast is clear," he says.

We all scurry out, then I reenter the master code to relock the door.

Molly already has her phone out, watching for the signal. "Still no— Oops, there it is! Wow, we *just* made it!"

The words are barely out of her mouth when a uniformed officer comes around the corner from Ruby Street.

"Hey!" he shouts. "What are you kids doing?"

7

Merry little Christmas

M

MY HEART LEAPS into my throat as we all turn to face the police officer.

"We... We, ah—" My mind goes blank as I try to stammer out some kind of excuse.

Swiftly, Molly speaks up. "We were on our way to the Christmas Eve Cantata at the church—" She points in that direction. "—when some crazy-acting guy with a gun tried to rob us. We managed to keep him talking for a little while—he was really rambling, probably on drugs or something—but then he yelled something about a spaceship and just ran off. We came to report what happened, but nobody's here." She indicates the sign on the door we saw this morning. "We were just about to call the number," she adds, holding up the phone still in her hand from checking the wi-fi signal.

With a quick, admiring glance at her, I nod. "Can you maybe tell someone? We're already super late to the Cantata and promised her mom and my aunt we'd be there. They're in the choir."

The officer frowns, looking skeptical. "Where did this happen?"

Tristan takes Molly's hand. "About a block from here, on Diamond Street," he says. "The guy was heading in the direction of the shopping district. We're afraid he might hurt someone."

The frown disappears and the officer smiles. "I appreciate you all coming by the station to report it. This town could use more kids like you. I'll contact the other officer on call and we'll try to find him. Thanks." Still smiling, he turns away to detach a radio from his belt and speak into it.

While he's doing that, Sean and Kira quickly pull the sticky note off the camera above the officer's head and flutter it to the ground behind his back.

I make a tiny motion with my head to the others and we all go down the steps to Onyx Street and turn toward the church. I glance back at the officer, who nods and waves us on. Relieved, we hurry away.

"Wow, that was close," Sean murmurs once we're well out of earshot. "Might be the tightest spot you guys have talked your way out of yet," he tells Molly and Tristan.

She stifles a laugh. "Don't forget pulling you all out of Devyn's mind control, weekend before last. That was maybe a *little* tighter?"

We all laugh then, because she's absolutely right. If she hadn't broken our thrall, that traitor would probably be in charge of the Council and everything else by now.

"Okay, second tightest," Sean concedes, grinning. The relief at having successfully pulled off our mission just now has made us all a little giddy.

I do my best to shake it off. "C'mon. If we're going to get back to the church before the Cantata is over, we need to hurry."

That gets everyone moving. Walking quickly toward the church, we strategize our next steps.

"At least the most time-sensitive part is done," Rigel says. "Now we don't have to worry about anyone else being hurt or killed by whatever's in this bag." He pats his coat pocket.

"Assuming it really is dangerous," Tristan says. "I mean, it's still *possible* the woman just had a heart attack, right?"

Rigel shrugs. "We'll know for sure once we check out the bag."

"That'll have to wait, though," Kira says. "We need to make it back before the service is over. Probably safest not to do it without better light, anyway."

"Definitely," I agree. "Since tomorrow's Christmas, and the bag's no longer a risk to anybody, why don't we wait till the day after to examine it? Then we can decide what to do next. Meanwhile, let's do our best to just enjoy the holiday."

The choir is singing their final song when we slip back into the sanctuary. Other latecomers took our vacated seats, so we stand quietly just inside the door for the final strains of "O Holy Night" and the pastor's Christmas benediction.

As the organist plays a medley of Christmas carols, the crowd slowly moves our way, exchanging holiday wishes as they go. We wait until our families rejoin us, our excuse ready in case they ask where we disappeared to. Fortunately, we don't need it.

"It's a shame you all didn't manage to get here a bit sooner," Mrs. O'Gara remarks as the whole group of us goes out into the frosty night air. "I was quite surprised by how quickly the church filled up."

"Yes, we originally tried to save seats for you all," Mr. Morain, Kira's dad, says, "but we soon realized that wasn't practical—or fair. I imagine you were able to hear everything from the back, though?"

We all nod, since we can't very well admit we only caught the beginning and end of the program.

Because I already agreed to ride home with my aunt and uncle, I give Rigel a quick goodbye kiss outside the church. "See you tomorrow."

"Can't wait," he says, grinning. *Till then,* he adds silently, *just remember I love you…more than anything!*

Ditto, I respond, infusing the word with the love I know he can sense—and which he sends back.

Warmed despite the cold, I follow my aunt and uncle to their car, thinking over this evening's events.

Despite a minor glitch or two, our plan went off surprisingly well. Now I just need to take my own advice and not worry about the next stage until after Christmas. It won't be easy, since the idea that someone, possibly right in Jewel, wants Rigel dead, is seriously disturbing.

But who knows? Maybe Ethel Ann really did die of a simple heart attack and the bag will turn out to be harmless after all, I tell myself as my uncle drives home.

Deep inside, though, I doubt it.

I wake the next morning to falling snow. Perfect for Christmas Day—though I hope it won't snow enough to keep Rigel and his folks from driving to the O'Garas' house later on.

A week ago, Mrs. O'Gara invited his family and mine for Christmas dinner, as well as Kira's and Tristan's. My aunt and uncle declined, Aunt Theresa saying she'd already invited a few church friends who would otherwise be alone today. I suspect she was also uncomfortable with the idea of being the only two *Duchas* in a houseful of Martians.

Christmas morning with my aunt and uncle is surprisingly pleasant, unlike most I remember growing up. Maybe because Aunt Theresa has become so much less resentful of me since learning my true identity? In years past, I always got the impression she only got me presents at all because it was expected. This year is different.

"You used to beg to have your ears pierced and I would never allow it," she says, handing me a small, wrapped package. "But you're nearly seventeen now, and hold a rather, ah, responsible position. So, if you'd still like to have that done…you may. If not, I can always exchange these for clip-ons."

Startled and touched, I remove the bow, take off the wrapping paper and open the little box. Nestled inside are a pair of earrings, each with three silver stars dangling from small wire hoops. "These are beautiful, Aunt Theresa! Thank you!"

She beams—not nearly as rare an expression as it used to be. "I thought these would complement that little pin you always wear. Didn't you say it was from Molly?"

"Yes." Looking again at the earrings, I see she's right. Molly had those pins made for all six members of our Bond Squad to be our "secret" symbol and show of unity. Maybe I should get matching earrings for Molly and Kira for their birthdays?

"They're perfect," I assure my aunt, leaning over to give her a hug. Since our frightening experience locked together in a meat cooler three months ago, I'm no longer afraid to do that.

Even so, her return hug is slightly awkward. I guess real change takes time.

After lunch, I help Aunt Theresa with the stuffing and roast veggies, then go upstairs to my room to brush my hair one last time and tie a ribbon around Rigel's present. I've done a pretty good job of not thinking about it when he might "hear" me, but now I'm nervous he'll think it's weird.

Fetching my coat, I tuck his present into my biggest pocket, call out a cheery goodbye to my aunt and uncle and walk the half block to the O'Garas' house. My Bodyguard Cormac—who also happens to be Jewel High's vice principal—follows about a hundred yards back, like he always does if Rigel's not around.

Just as I get to the O'Garas' house, Rigel and his parents drive up.

"Merry Christmas," I call out as they get out of their car. Dr. and Mr. Stuart echo my greeting and together we all troop up to the front porch.

As his parents ring the bell, Rigel hangs back to give me a quick kiss. Then, hazel eyes twinkling, he says, "This Christmas should be way better than last year's, don't you think?"

Despite the potential threat still hanging over him, I have to agree. A year ago, our holidays were both stressful and awkward, with me bound by my promise to the Council to pretend I was dating Sean instead of Rigel. He and I did manage to sneak a couple of brief moments alone over winter break, but he's right. This year is *way* better.

We follow the Stuarts inside, where the O'Gara's small living room—the same size as ours—is already crowded. A festively decorated Christmas tree fills one corner and both kitchen and dining room chairs have been pressed into service to accommodate the four Morains, Tristan and his mother, the O'Garas and now us.

Holiday greetings are exchanged as Mrs. O passes around a huge plate of Christmas cookies. "Now, do you young people want to exchange gifts before or after we eat?" she asks. "The turkey and ham are already sliced and ready. Not to worry, dear," she assures Kira's little sister. "I have a nice salmon filet for you, as well."

Adina smiles her gratitude. After growing up in Nuath, where all meat is synthesized from animal cells, the only "real" kind of meat she's comfortable eating is fish.

"Let's eat now," Sean suggests, surprising no one. "Uh, then we can take our time with the presents."

Probably because of the mouth-watering smells wafting from the kitchen, nobody objects. Rather than let Cormac and Gilda stand guard outside, we invite them in to join us. They reluctantly come in, but insist on eating in the kitchen. I only agree because fourteen people are already a lot to squeeze into the O'Garas' small dining room, though we manage somehow.

The food is even more delicious than it smells. The conversation is lively but a little hard to follow, so many people are talking at once. Occasionally Rigel and I resort to communicating silently, and from the expressions I sometimes catch on the other two bonded couples' faces, we're not the only ones.

A good hour and a half later, even Sean has finished, after two extra helpings of pie—there are three, pumpkin, apple and mincemeat. Finally, we all push back from the table.

"If you young people will carry the dishes into the kitchen," Mrs. O says, "we grownups can do the washing up while you have your own little Christmas."

We all jump up to shuttle plates, bowls and platters into the kitchen, then go back to the living room, where we all left our gifts under the tree. My nervousness about what Rigel will think of mine, forgotten for a while, now returns. I can tell Rigel's nervous again, too—for the same reason.

Because of that, we both hang back as the other two couples exchange their gifts. Sean and Kira give each other little scrolls to open—but though it's obvious they're both very touched by whatever they read inside, they refuse to share with the rest of us.

Tristan gives Molly a pretty bracelet of linked stars to match our pins, which reminds me of the earrings Aunt Theresa gave me. I'll get my ears pierced after the holidays, so I can show them off.

My insecurity ramps up several more notches when I see Molly's present to Tristan—a flash drive containing a song she wrote herself. He wants to play it immediately, but she demurs.

"Later, okay? I'd rather you hear it the first time when it's just us."

That gives me an idea. "Um, you want to do our gift exchange out on the porch?" I ask Rigel.

I can sense his relief at the suggestion. "Great idea. We'll be back in a few minutes," he tells the others, who are now so wrapped up in each other they barely notice.

It's freezing out, but since no *Duchas* are around to notice, I don't hesitate to use the climate control app on my omni-phone to keep us warm—though I barely need it while sitting next to Rigel on the porch swing. Compared to Molly's, my present feels lamer than ever. I give it to him right away rather than prolong my anxiety.

Smiling, he unwraps it to reveal a little leather folder embossed with stars.

"Wow, M, this is really pretty." Then he opens it and falls silent, his brows going up. I hold my breath as he reads what's inside. Finally, his eye suspiciously bright, he looks at me. "Did you write this yourself?"

I nod. "I didn't set it to music or anything, but… Do you like it?"

In answer, he folds me into his arms. "I love it," he whispers. "I can't believe you wrote a whole sonnet just for me."

He then hands me a tiny wrapped box. "This seems almost impersonal in comparison, but I hope you'll like it, too."

I untie the ribbon, tear off the paper and open the box. Inside is a gold chain with two glass spheres dangling from it. Looking closer, I see one is a tiny replica of Mars and the other of the planet Earth.

"Wow," I breathe. "This is beautiful!"

His grin is relieved. "I'm glad you like it. It…seemed appropriate, you know?"

I throw my arms around his neck. "I love it! Thank you! This is the reason you were at Glitterby's?"

He nods. "No idea how someone found out I'd ordered it, but they must have to…you know. Unless they just saw my name on that sticker and acted on impulse?"

A sudden chill makes me shiver despite my climate control app. "Let's not think about that right now, okay? Today is for happiness, and family."

"And love," he murmurs, leaning over for another kiss. "Merry Christmas, M."

8

Naughty or nice

Rigel

THE DAY AFTER CHRISTMAS, I wake with a smile, fresh from an awesome dream about M. Not until I'm getting dressed do I remember what's on the agenda for today—finding out whether someone tried to kill me or not.

You awake? I think to M before going downstairs to breakfast.

Yep, she instantly sends back. *When and where do you want to do this?*

I think for a moment. *How about here, this afternoon? My folks will be out for a couple hours then. If it turns out to be…what we think, I can ask my mom to have it analyzed as soon as they get back.*

Good plan, she agrees. *I'll let the others know.*

A few hours later, our six-person Bond Squad gathers around my kitchen table. My parents are both at NuAgra—Mom to help a new Healer get settled and Dad to make a few last-minute tweaks to the new *Echtran* communication and streaming network he created. It's supposed to go live planet-wide on New Year's Day.

I've already set the "evidence" we stole from the police station in the middle of the table—the red cellophane beignet package in a zipped plastic bag. For a long moment, we all just stare at it. Then I clear my throat. "Ready?" I ask.

Everyone nods.

"This'll be a bit of a letdown if it turns out to be nothing after all," Sean comments, though without the snark in his tone he'd have used a year ago.

"Not to me." M eyes the innocent-looking parcel with something almost like horror. "I'll be massively relieved. Open it, Rigel—but be really, *really* careful!"

I unseal the outer bag, then let Sean and Kira levitate out the inner one containing the possibly-poisoned beignets so no one has to touch it. Then, using two forks, I cautiously pull apart the edges of the cellophane bag, examining it carefully for anything out of the ordinary.

"What are those?" Molly asks, pointing.

I lean closer and see what look like two tiny needles on opposite sides of the open top of the bag. "Huh. Glad I didn't use my fingers just now. Not exactly standard gift-bag features, are they?"

"Definitely not," M agrees. She carefully lifts the bag—from the bottom—to examine the top edges more closely. "I'm betting these are filled with that toxin, and that's what killed Ethel Ann."

The sight of M that close to something that deadly tightens my throat. Reaching over, I take the bag back, nearly dropping it in the process. "Oops!"

M and the others all gasp. "Rigel!" she exclaims. "You didn't—it didn't—?"

"No, no," I reassure her. "Neither needle touched me." But I'm quick to set the bag down again. "So it really was murder. The killer just got the wrong target."

"Now what?" Tristan asks.

Kira frowns. "Now that we know, shouldn't we turn it over to the *Echtran* Council and their security folks? They have more resources to go after a killer than we do."

"Given the, um, special advantages we have, I'm not sure that's true," I reply. "But I guess we should accept any help we can get to catch them. There's no knowing if I was their only target." I slide a worried glance M's way to see her looking back with a similar expression.

"I agree," she says. "Let's show this to your mom as soon as she gets home. If she can't analyze whatever's on those needles herself, I'm sure there's someone at NuAgra who can. Then I'll contact Kyna to let her know, too."

In response to her questioning look, I nod. "Right. I didn't want to bring the Council into it on just a hunch, but now it looks like my hunch was right."

Leaving the bag where it is, I go to the fridge and get sodas for everyone while they start speculating on who might have tried to kill me. I can tell the topic makes M really uncomfortable, but she joins in anyway, like the Sovereign she is.

"We still don't know exactly how many people with questionable political views live in this part of Indiana," she points out. "I'm sure there are at least a few, and there could be a lot more. We also don't know if this attempt was made by a lone radical, or as part of some larger conspiracy, maybe involving Devyn Kane himself. I doubt he's completely abandoned his ambitions just because we blew up his Ossian Sphere a couple weeks ago."

That produces an uncomfortable murmur from the rest of us. If a bunch of people are colluding, any or all of us could be their next potential victim. Maybe I just provided the first convenient opportunity when they spotted that package in Glitterby's clearly labeled with my name.

"M and I can try scanning as wide an area around Jewel as possible for hostile vibes," I suggest. "But even if we find some really bad ones, we won't know for sure it's the murderer."

"It's a place to start, though." Tristan darts a concerned look Molly's way, no doubt remembering the attempt on *her* life several weeks back. "Why don't you do that now?"

I look at M and she shrugs.

"Might as well," she says. "Ready, Rigel?"

In answer, I take her hand firmly in mine and put my other arm around her shoulders. *Let's see what we can find,* I think to her.

After a couple of deep, centering breaths, M stretches out with her special ability. Linked as we are, physically and mentally, I'm aware of everything she senses. Because my house is in a sparsely populated farming area, it takes a few minutes to push her perception far enough out to pick up anything beyond a few regular *Duchas* going about their business.

Then her probing reaches the outskirts of downtown Jewel, where there are a lot more emotions to sift through, some of them now *Echtran*. None feel particularly negative, other than occasional mild irritation over something or other.

"I'll check NuAgra," she murmurs aloud, still concentrating. "Some of our people still live there. Then I'll expand to nearby towns. Might take a while…"

By the time she's scanned NuAgra and its surroundings, I can tell she's getting tired. I take her other hand in my free one to double our skin-to-skin contact, which has helped in the past. Then I feel a hand on my wrist. Glancing over in surprise, I see Molly, her other hand in Tristan's, who quickly links to Kira and Sean, as well. Immediately, M's power increases at least six-fold.

Thanks, she sends mentally to the whole group. *I should have suggested this to begin with.*

Her augmented abilities now allow her to push farther, faster. Soon she's picking up emotions from Alexandria, then Elwood. In both, M senses distinctive *Echtran* vibes, a few on the distinctly unpleasant side. Casting wider, she finds a few more in towns slightly farther away. Finally, when she's covered a circle that must be close to a hundred miles in diameter, she lets go with a sigh.

"Thanks, guys," she says, aloud this time. "That helped a whole lot. There are definitely some people within easy driving distance who could be suspects. Totally possible one of them did this." She nods at the cellophane bag on the table. "Unfortunately, we can't haul people in for questioning just for giving off negative vibes, even if we knew who they were."

"Yeah, I don't know if I feel better or worse now that you've confirmed we definitely have baddies in the area," Tristan admits. "But better to know than not, right?"

Before she can answer, the door from the garage opens and my parents walk in. "Hello, everyone," Mom says cheerily. "Rigel mentioned you might be stopping by."

"I'm glad you're all here." Dad's smiling, too. "Especially M and Molly, er, the Sovereign and Princess—"

"M and Molly's fine," Molly quickly puts in. She's still a little uncomfortable with her title. Not surprising. It took M months to get used to hers.

Dad's smile broadens. "M and Molly, then. You'll be happy to hear that your proposal for a regular weekly broadcast has been approved. Carleen, the program director, has an open Thursday evening slot that's yours, if you want it. She said you can record your first episode as soon as you're willing. The new network is slated to go live on New Year's Day, just six days from now—which happens to be a Thursday."

M and Molly exchange wide-eyed stares. They didn't expect approval to come so quickly—or maybe at all.

"What do you think?" M asks Molly, who gives a little shrug.

"Why not? If we're gonna do this, we may as well jump straight in, don't you think?"

"You're right. Why waste time?" M agrees. "There are obviously lots of minds that still need to be changed—some of them way too close to Jewel for comfort."

Mom and Dad both frown. "Why do you say that?" Dad asks.

"Because of what happened a couple days before Christmas," I tell them. I go on to relate what happened at Glitterby's and the needles we just discovered, though I leave out the part about us breaking into the police station. Fortunately, they don't ask how we got hold of the evidence. Yet.

Picking up one of the forks I used earlier, I point out the two tiny needles we discovered in the bag's opening. "We're hoping either Mom or someone she knows can analyze those needles for us," I finish.

Leaning closer, my mom gasps. "Those look like miniature versions of the ampules I keep in my bag for quick administration of injectables. *Echtran*-made ampules!"

"That's what we thought," M says. "Which means Ethel Ann was killed by an *Echtran*."

"But...why?" Dad looks confused. "Why would one of our people want to murder a *Duchas*?"

M puts a hand on my arm before I blurt out the answer. "Maybe you should both sit down," she suggests.

Clearly baffled, Mom and Dad take the chairs Sean and Kira quickly offer them.

"Rigel thinks," M continues, "we all think, that whatever killed Ethen Ann was intended for someone else."

Both of my parents look at me and I nod. "Yep. Me. I didn't want freak you guys out before we were sure, but this bag was supposed to have been mine. It was sitting on top of M's present at Glitterby's, waiting for me to pick it up. Had a sticker on it with my name, big as life. Ethel Ann was being obnoxious, so Agatha gave the bag to her instead, to shut her up. Otherwise..."

Mom regards the otherwise-innocent-looking little gift bag with horror. "Otherwise you would have— Oh, Rigel!" With a sob, she throws her arms around me.

"It's okay, Mom." I awkwardly pat her on the back, acutely aware of everyone watching. "I'm fine."

"You're right, we need to have those needles analyzed," Dad says, frowning again. "Confirm they contain an *Echtran*-made toxin."

Drawing back, Mom nods, tears still shimmering in her eyes. "I'll take it to Healer Nialls at NuAgra. He's better versed in toxicology than I am and has the proper equipment there. But...how did you get this?" She motions at the bag. "I assume it was left at Glitterby's after the medics took Ethel Ann away?"

I glance at M. "Er—"

"That's not important now," M says quickly—and authoritatively. "What matters is proving an *Echtran* did this, then catching that person so they can't make another attempt. Rigel might not be so lucky a second time."

"Of course." Straightening, Mom pulls out her phone. "I'll contact Nialls now to see if he's available."

While she taps out a quick message, Dad gets a large glass jar out of a cabinet, puts on a glove to carefully place the beignet package inside and tightly closes the lid. "Let's make sure this can't hurt anyone else, shall we?"

Then, turning to M and Molly, he adds, "We don't dare assume Rigel is the only one at risk from whoever did this. Excellencies, I strongly urge you both to consider moving into your quarters at NuAgra until that person is apprehended. The security there is substantially better than anything I was able to install at your homes."

Clearly caught off guard, they both blink at him.

"We haven't even confirmed our suspicion that those needles contain a toxin yet," M points out.

That gets a smile from Dad. "I, and the rest of the Council, have learned the hard way not to discount your suspicions, even before they're confirmed."

He's referring, I know, to M's and my insistence that the Council needed to cancel the recent NuAgra tour and dedication based on what they considered a wild theory…that turned out to be right.

"Ariel, has Nialls responded yet?"

She glances at her phone. "Yes, he says he's at NuAgra now. I'll run this over to him right away." She puts the sealed jar into her black medical bag.

The rest of us stand up.

"Guess there's not much else we can do till we get those results back," I say.

M rode here with Molly and Tristan, but I offer to drive her back myself—it'll give us a brief chance to be alone. Molly and Tristan will probably appreciate some privacy, too, since we're all still a little shaken.

"See?" I say once M and I are in my car. "I'm not the only one who thinks you could also be a target." I put a hand over hers on the console to communicate my love and worry more strongly.

"When have I ever stopped being a target?" She attempts a little laugh. "Being a leader means having enemies. Goes with the territory. Anyway, you know darned well it's only because of me that someone went after you. *I'm* the one who put *you* in danger. Again."

I tighten my grip on her hand. "My life wouldn't mean anything at all without you, M. Being together is worth any risk to *me*, but I hate to think of you in danger."

"And I feel exactly the same way," she solemnly assures me. "We both let our guard down after foiling Devyn's plan, which was a mistake. Going forward, we'll both need to be more vigilant."

"No kidding." I reluctantly let go of her hand since I need both of mine to back out of the driveway.

"You'll keep me posted on that analysis, right?" she says as I head toward downtown.

I nod. "Of course, though it'll probably be tomorrow before we get the results."

Before I drop M off, we indulge in a nice, long makeout session a block from her house. Knowing how close we came to losing each other forever adds extra passion to our kisses. Unfortunately, we never seem to get enough privacy to do *more* than kiss. Or maybe fortunately? Either way, saying goodbye is harder than ever when I finally pull into her driveway.

"This incident has made me realize just how easy it could be for someone to…you know," I tell her.

"Same here," she says. "But you and I have faced a lot of threats over the past year and a half. Like all the others, we can handle this one, too—as long as we're together."

I smile. "You're right. I love you, M."

She leans over to give me one last kiss. "I love you, too, Rigel. See you soon."

9

Let's look at the show

M

THE NEXT DAY I'm extra grateful Rigel and I stole that lovely bit of alone time, since I turn out to be so busy, I never get to see him at all.

I'm still finishing breakfast when Molly shows up to brainstorm the initial segment of our new broadcast.

"Dad says the program director wants to meet with us today," she tells me across a plate of my aunt's homemade cinnamon rolls. "So we should probably have at least a rough idea of what we want to do with this show. The main point will be to sway people away from Devyn and his radicals, toward you and the Council, right?"

"*Us* and the Council," I correct her. "Right. I seem to be making a *little* progress with my *Echtran Enquirer* columns, according to the most recent polls. But with murderous types still living right here in Indiana, we obviously need to do a lot more."

Molly takes a thoughtful sip of milk. "Wish we knew exactly how many—and how murderous. Do you think Mum and Mr. Stuart are right that we should more or less move to NuAgra?"

"Like I told Rigel yesterday, there will always be *some* threats out there. We'll never get absolutely everyone's support, no matter how persuasive we are. And think how awkward that would be once school starts back up."

Molly grimaces. "Good point. Not to mention how much harder it would be to get private time with our guys. They probably wouldn't even be allowed in our quarters without chaperones. Mum, at least, would likely insist on a rule like that. She's all about appearances."

"Also a good point. Living there would be almost like living in a fishbowl. So we're agreed? No panic move to NuAgra?"

"Agreed. Hopefully they'll catch whoever tried to poison Rigel soon," she says. "Anyway, our first broadcast?"

We spend all morning jotting down ideas, then continue over lunch at Molly's house. By the time Mr. O'Gara drives us out to NuAgra to meet with the *Echtran* News Network's program director, we've sketched out an opening segment to introduce ourselves and our goals to the viewers. Who, if Mr. Stuart is right, will include more than eighty percent of our people on Earth, as well as the majority of those on Mars.

We're nearly to NuAgra when Rigel reaches out mentally to let me know his mother's Healer friend ran a chemical analysis and confirmed those needles in the beignet bag were filled with a deadly toxin.

Dad's already told Kyna, he tells me, *so I'm guessing there'll be some discussion about it at your Council meeting tonight. Or are they skipping it because of the holidays?*

No, but it was supposed to be a short one. This news might change that. Thanks, Rigel.

I relay the news to Molly and her dad, who's obviously hearing about this for the first time.

"Someone attempted to poison Rigel?" Slowing the van to a halt at NuAgra's manned gate, he glances back at us. "When?"

We wait till the guard bows and waves us through, then explain what happened at Glitterby's before Christmas and what we discovered yesterday. Again, we gloss over exactly how we obtained the beignet bag, letting him assume Rigel snagged it the day of the murder.

Mr. O pulls into a parking spot near the main doors. "If there's a killer around, the two of you should be better protected," he says, echoing what Mr. Stuart said yesterday. "Your quarters here at NuAgra—"

"No, Dad," Molly interrupts. "Neither of us want to move here, not yet. We've already discussed it. Besides," she adds, with an air of clinching it, "those apartments aren't exactly ready to move into. I still need to pick out furniture, color schemes, everything. I've been looking forward to that."

I stifle a laugh. In her own way, Molly cares as much about appearances as Mrs. O does—one thing that made her a great Hand-maid before we discovered she's actually a Princess. Personally, I'm way more worried about guaranteed alone time with Rigel than furniture styles.

Though I expect Mr. O to argue as we get out of the car, he lets the subject drop—just one more indication of the increased respect Molly gets from her adoptive parents now that they know her real identity. While they always treated her way better than my Aunt Theresa used to treat me, they never quite let her forget she was supposedly from a lower *fine* than theirs. Which turned out not to be true at all.

Preceding Molly and her dad to the frosted glass entry doors, I press my palm against the access panel. It registers my DNA and the doors hiss open—a nearly foolproof method to prevent unauthorized access by non-Martians. As we advance into the big, open lobby area, a handsome brunette woman with close-cropped hair comes forward and bows, right fist over heart.

"Hello, Excellencies," she greets us. "Thank you for coming. I'm Carleen, ENN Program Director. I thought we should discuss the format of your program and work out recording and broadcast schedules. Would you like to see the studio?"

We both nod.

"This way." She turns and walks briskly away, leaving us no

choice but to follow. I glance at Molly, who looks as intimidated as I am by the woman's air of energetic, professional efficiency.

Near the back of the reception area, she turns down a hallway, opens a door and ushers us inside. I look around at what appears to be a comfy little living room on a small stage, with tiny cameras and microphones positioned around it. It reminds me of the sets I visited in Nuath, when I was doing all those interviews to persuade people to emigrate to Earth.

"You can change the furnishings to your tastes, of course," Colleen informs us. "We have a variety of chairs and sofas in various styles and colors to give the illusion that each program is recorded in a different room. For now, however, this is our only interview setup. This particular configuration will be for Gwendolyn Gannett's weekly broadcast."

Molly and I both cringe at the name.

"So she really is going to have her own show?" Molly asks.

Colleen's brows go up in surprise. "Of course. As Gwendolyn is already a household name to most *Echtrans*, she's bound to be a big ratings draw. I imagine the two of you will be, as well. Gwendolyn has requested Tuesday evenings for her slot, to coincide with the weekly *Echtran Enquirer* release."

Neither of us are happy about that, but we don't argue.

"Will Thursday evenings work for both of you?" Colleen asks. "We can be fairly flexible as to when we record your broadcasts, though we'd prefer at least a day ahead of airing. Unless you prefer to broadcast live? Gwendolyn has indicated she'll pre-record all of hers."

Feeling slightly overwhelmed, I glance at Molly again. "Mostly recorded, I think?" Molly nods. "And Thursdays are fine."

"Later, we, ah, thought we might sometimes do a live lead-in," Molly adds, "then go to a recorded interview or something, if that works?"

Colleen smiles, which suddenly makes her look much more approachable. "Certainly, if you like. My job, and my staff's, is to provide you with whatever you need. Now, were you thinking an hour-long slot, or just a half hour? I can work our other programming around either one."

"Half an hour will be fine," I assure her. "Especially to start out." Molly and I agreed that filling a whole hour every week could quickly turn into a lot of work.

Over the next hour-plus, Colleen discusses various other production details with us. Molly also shares her ideas for how our set should look—totally different from Gwendolyn's overstuffed, bright florals—after which Colleen leads us back to the main hall.

"If you'll excuse me now, Excellencies, I have quite a lot to accomplish before our inaugural broadcast on New Year's Day. I'll see you again on Tuesday, when you come back to record your first broadcast. Thank you for taking the time to talk with me today." With a parting bow, she hurries off.

We return to the main lobby area, but don't see Mr. O—which seems to please Molly.

"Come on," she says. "What with bombs and conspiracy theorists and explosions in the sky, you still haven't seen our quarters here. You're not going to believe how big they are."

She proceeds to drag me off to my new suite of rooms, which is every bit as extensive as she'd described.

"See?" She grins at my stunned expression. "And mine's just as humongous. Crazy, huh? Though there's definitely no way we'd want to live here yet. I mean, just look at this stuff." Molly glares at the sturdy desk, conference table and utilitarian chairs in the two front rooms, then the similarly functional bedroom set in the personal area.

"And mine is *exactly* the same," she informs me. "No character or personality at all. They might as well put us in prison!"

I don't point out that these bedrooms are three times the size of ours at home, since I also have zero desire to move here. Certainly not without Rigel, or at least some guarantee of regular private time with him. I'm already feeling a little twitchy after just twenty-four hours apart.

"Just wait till I have a chance to do these rooms up properly, though," Molly continues, grinning again. "It'll be almost like being back in Nuath."

I gaze around. Despite the generic furnishings, the space *is* reminiscent of my Sovereign quarters in the Royal Palace on Mars. "There's no hurry, though, right? We already agreed we won't move out here anytime soon."

"Not *soon*, no. But maybe in a year and a half, after we graduate? Um, if we both stay on Earth, that is."

Startled, I briefly probe her feelings. "You don't want to?"

She shrugs. "Tristan's never been to Nuath, you know. And his mother's been wanting to go back, though she's obviously happier here than she used to be."

"But you never—" I break off at the sound of Mr. O'Gara calling our names. "I guess we have plenty of time to figure it all out before the next launch window. C'mon."

We hurry back out to the reception area, where Mr. O is waiting.

"Lili just called to say tonight's Council meeting has been moved earlier, to five o'clock," he tells us. "Did you see that they've now furnished your new quarters?"

"If you want to call it that." Molly rolls her eyes. "We're even more sure now that we're not moving here right away!"

Though I can sense Mr. O's disappointment and concern, he again doesn't try to argue. "We still have nearly an hour until the meeting," he says instead. "Why don't we get a snack? I don't believe either of you have seen NuAgra's cafeteria yet."

He leads us to the dining area, which reminds me of those on the ships I took to and from Mars last spring and summer. "Are those—?"

"Yes, the recombinators just came online yesterday," Mr. O proudly informs us. "Right now the selection is fairly limited, but as we continue to stock their stores, they'll expand substantially. We also plan to install one in each of your quarters."

"Nice!" Molly exclaims. "I've missed those. Maybe living here won't be *so* awful—eventually. After I totally redo our quarters."

Not having grown up with things like food recombinators, I don't share Molly's nostalgia for them. In fact, the longer I can put off trading my normal Earthlike existence for a more official Martian one, the better, in my opinion.

After a light snack of fruit, cheese and chips in the cafeteria, Molly and I head to the new *Echtran* Council room where our weekly meetings now take place. It's a lot bigger than the O'Garas' living room.

The rest of the Council is already seated in cushy chairs around the conference table when we arrive. Kyna, the Council leader, and little Nara are here holographically, as usual, since both women live in Washington, DC, where Kyna is a NASA astrophysicist and Nara is a microbiologist at the World Health Organization, specializing in pediatrics.

At our entrance, everyone stands and bows. Though that still bothers Molly, especially when Mrs. O'Gara bows to her, she's getting better at hiding her discomfort.

"Thank you for accommodating the earlier hour, Excellencies," Kyna says. "I thought it necessary, given this unsettling new development."

At questioning looks from the others, she explains about the attempt on Rigel's life, including the accidental but unfortunate death of a local *Duchas*. "Healer Nialls has confirmed with a counterpart in Dun Cloch that the toxin is the identical substance the radicals have used previously. Concerning, to say the least."

"I'll say," I agree. "Where are they getting this stuff? Who makes it? Do they have an unlimited supply?"

Kyna favors me with a grim smile. "I asked precisely those questions after Enid's suicide, Excellency, and we finally have some answers. It seems a Chemist in Dun Cloch manufactured it on orders from Lach Lennox more than a year ago. He claims to have created only one batch, but admitted it was a rather large one."

"Do we have any idea how much is still unaccounted for?" I ask, with a sense of *dejà vú*. "Maybe this stuff can't level whole buildings, like that antimatter we destroyed, but it's pretty darned devastating on an individual level—and just as easy to conceal."

"Easier, actually," Mr. Stuart says. "Antimatter emits a signal that we can scan for."

Kyna glances down at her tablet with a frown. "Our Chemists are working on an antidote and our Engineers on some kind of detection device, but as neither is available yet, we must all be on our guard."

Everyone shifts uncomfortably in their chairs.

"On a slightly different note," Kyna says, looking around the table, "Breann informs me that I'm not the only one who has finally remembered the details of what happened here two weeks ago?"

As most of the others nod, Molly and I exchange an uneasy glance. *Uh-oh.*

"Yes," says Breann, a beautiful brunette who looks like she's in her twenties but is actually well past sixty. "Though finally recalling everything that occurred that evening has raised some, ah, questions about the explanation we were initially given."

"Indeed." Kyna raises an eyebrow at Molly and me. "I clearly remember the appearance of an Ossian Sphere, Devyn Kane's hologram, and how he used the Sphere to exert control over us all. Also that we came perilously close to naming him both *Echtran* Regent and leader of this Council before he was *somehow* dissuaded and the Sphere destroyed."

Malcolm, one of the four Royals on the Council, leans forward. "That's what I recall, too. But how were the Sovereign and Princess Malena able to use Royal "push" on a mere hologram? That should not have been possible."

Kyna is frowning now. "No. Nor did Devyn act as though he'd been convinced of anything. Instead, he became quite angry just before vanishing."

"We, ah…" I begin to stammer, looking to Molly for inspiration since she's better than I am at making stuff up on the fly.

Then Nara speaks up. "I seem to remember all of the young people linking hands shortly before the Sphere moved out of range and Devyn's hologram disappeared."

"Nara is right," Kyna says. "It looked as though the six of you somehow worked together to banish the Sphere to a safe distance. But how?"

I give Molly a resigned little shrug. We did warn the rest of our Bond Squad this might happen, and they agreed we should tell the complete truth if it did. Molly nods and I turn to face the Council.

"It, ah, turns out Rigel and I aren't the only couple who have formed a *graell* bond," I tell them. "Over the past month or so, it's become obvious that Molly and Tristan have one, too."

Teara, Tristan's mom, gives a small gasp and looks wonderingly at Molly. Mrs. O'Gara stares at her, too.

"So do Sean and Kira," I add.

Mrs. O's disbelieving expression is suddenly tinged with outrage. "What? Impossible! That can't possibly be true. Can it?"

"It's true, Mum." Molly holds her mother's gaze so Mrs. O can verify her words with her special lie-detector ability. "Sean and Kira are well and truly *graell* bonded, and so are Tristan and I."

Though she must know Molly's telling the truth, Mrs. O still looks skeptical. "But…but…they're from different *fines*!"

"Rigel and I are from different *fines*, too," I remind her.

"See? So it's obviously not impossible," Molly points out reasonably. "Anyway, if it weren't for that telekinesis thing Sean and Kira's *graell* can do, we never could have pushed the Ossian Sphere far enough away to explode it safely."

Everyone looks totally flabbergasted now, so I quickly back Molly up. "She's right. You know how Rigel and I can generate electricity and talk telepathically? Well, since bonding, the other two couples have also started developing special abilities. Different ones."

"But…telekinesis?" Mr. Stuart looks almost dazed. "I've never… How—?"

"I'd never heard of such a thing either," I agree, "but I've seen it with my own eyes, more than once. It only works if they're holding hands—just like Rigel's and my lightning thing."

Kyna looks from me to Molly and back, clearly struggling to absorb this new information. "Then… all six of you somehow *combined* powers to destroy the Ossian Sphere?"

"Yes," I confirm. "We'd discovered earlier that day that if we're all touching, every couple's abilities are enhanced. Which turned out to be an awfully good thing that night."

There's a murmur of agreement, but also much shaking of heads.

"I'm afraid I still don't understand," Malcolm complains. "Why weren't we told any of this before?"

Little Nara chuckles. "Isn't that obvious? Look how you're all reacting! If you recall, Shim Stuart once suggested *graell* bonds might be more common than generally believed. It appears he was right."

She then turns excitedly to Molly and me. "I don't blame you a bit for keeping this secret, Excellencies, but now I'd *very* much like to learn more about what you can do! Singly, as couples, and as a group."

"I'm sure we all would," Kyna drily agrees, "in due time. Back to the incident in question, our security team in Dun Cloch has gleaned a fair bit of information from the three men we apprehended that evening. As we suspected, they were sent by Devyn Kane." Her mouth twists with distaste.

"Am I right that they smuggled the Ossian Sphere into the NuAgra grounds while my security systems were briefly disabled by that electromagnetic pulse?" Mr. Stuart asks.

Kyna nods. "An omni in their possession had been in recent contact with Devyn. That is apparently how he remotely controlled the Sphere and, through that, us."

"Except for my Molly." Mrs. O sends a fond glance her way. "And the Sovereign."

That compels me to admit, "Actually, he got to me, too. Molly was the only one immune—her new special power. When she grabbed my hand, she shared that immunity with me, then the rest of our group, once we were all touching. That let us all combine forces to neutralize the Sphere and destroy it."

As an approving murmur goes around the table, I smile at Molly. All things considered, telling the Council the whole truth—most of it, anyway—went a lot better than we expected. Hopefully we'll still be able to keep a *few* things secret, like our group telepathy while touching and the full extent of everyone's powers. Which still seem to be increasing.

"Did they learn anything else from those men?" Breann asks

then. "Such as how many followers Devyn has now, where they're located, and how well organized they are?"

"The inquiry is still ongoing," Kyna replies, 'but it appears Devyn has a larger following than we believed, probably several hundred strong. Worse, several apparently live uncomfortably close to Jewel, though none within the town limits."

"We were afraid of that," Mr. Stuart says, frowning. "I take it we don't have actual identities or addresses yet?"

Breann shakes her head. "No, though we've begun reviewing the applications of those who applied to live in Jewel but were not selected. Because Jewel is so small, many were disqualified on very minor grounds, simply to keep the number of new residents manageable. After this attempt on young Stuart's life, we'll look even more closely at their previous activities and political leanings."

"Please do," Kyna says. "Our interrogators have confirmed that Devyn has indeed created a loose alliance between at least three distinct groups of malcontents—former Faxon adherents, radical Populists and extreme Traditionalists who disapprove of some of our Sovereign's, ah, choices."

"Like Rigel." I give a little snort. "Uber-Traditionalists can be as dangerous as any Faxon supporter. Just ask Kira."

Several people wince at that reminder of how Allister Adair and Lach Lennox, two formerly high-ranking Royals, tried to use Kira as a human bomb to kill both me and Rigel.

"With so many potential enemies about," Mrs. O says, "surely it would be best for our Sovereign and Princess to remain at NuAgra for the present."

Molly and I exchange an exasperated look.

"This latest attempt wasn't even aimed at either of us," Molly protests.

"She's right," I agree. "And what kind of leader would I be, if I stayed barricaded in here while telling all our new immigrants to integrate with Earth society? And what's the point of all the extra security Mr. Stuart added to our houses, if we aren't going to live in them?"

Kyna sighs. "I suppose we can't insist. Though at the very least, you two and Rigel Stuart should absent yourselves from this week's planned holiday party. Or perhaps it would be best to cancel it entirely. The invitation was general, so every *Echtran* who can will likely attend—which could include whoever murdered that poor *Duchas*. A party of that sort would provide an ideal opportunity for that dissident to make another attempt on young Stuart's life—or someone else's."

"Or…a perfect opportunity to catch the murderer!" I exclaim, on sudden inspiration. "Kyna, I think we should not only go ahead with the party, we should let everyone know that Rigel will be there, along with both of us."

When Kyna looks skeptical, Molly backs me up. "M's right. And if someone were to, ah, 'leak' the guest list to Gwendolyn Gannett, let her think it's some kind of scoop—"

"She'd be guaranteed to publish it in Tuesday's *Echtran Enquirer*, the day before the party," I finish with a grin, remembering how Molly used that same trick to control the public narrative after we destroyed Devyn's Ossian Sphere. "Since whoever tried to kill Rigel can't possibly know we're onto them, they'll think it's a perfect chance to try again. If they do…we'll be ready for them."

10

Better not pout

Rigel

"WHAT?" Mom exclaims, clearly aghast, when Dad relates the details of the Council meeting after getting home. "They want to use our son as *bait* for this murderer? Van, don't tell me you agreed to this!"

"Mom, it's fine," I assure her. M already filled me in by having me "listen in" on the plan while she outlined it to the rest of the Council. "Way safer than *not* catching them. That would give them who knows how many chances to go after who knows how many people in the future."

Dad puts a calming hand on Mom's arm. "He's right, Ariel. The Sovereign seems confident that she and Rigel will be able to identify the person who did this if they attend the New Year's Eve party. She explained that together, they have a unique ability to gauge emotions and intent in others."

I nod. "It's how we discovered the Grentl in orbit in September. M told Kyna at the time, but she agreed we shouldn't publicize that particular power because it wouldn't be as useful if everyone knew about it. Um, sorry, Dad."

"No, no," he says. "I completely agree with Kyna's reasoning. But I must say, I was extremely glad to hear about this particular ability, as it provides an added level of security for you both that I was previously unaware of."

"Well, I can't do it on my own," I admit. "It's strictly M's special power. It's just stronger and easier when we're together. Um, touching."

Mom and Dad exchange a look I don't have any trouble interpreting, even without M's emotion-sensing thing.

"Just holding hands is enough," I explain and they both relax noticeably. "Something we can do at this party without making anyone suspicious. Honestly, Mom, this should be almost foolproof. At least if that person comes. Which they probably will. They can't know we found out what they tried to do. What do the *Duchas* doctors think that woman died from? Did you check on that, Mom?"

"Yes, I looked at Ms. Riverton's records earlier today," she says. "The physician on duty when she was brought in—already dead— put the cause down as a sudden, massive heart attack, though the police have requested an autopsy."

I roll my eyes. "Because of the gossip about Agatha Payton poisoning her?"

"Probably," Mom replies. "However, they do need permission from her next of kin, a niece who is currently out of the country, so it may be delayed a while."

"I doubt it will matter," Dad says. "When this toxin was used before, even our own Healers believed the victims died of natural causes—heart attacks. It's extremely doubtful any *Duchas* doctor will suspect otherwise."

Just like M predicted. "See?" I say to Mom. "Whoever did this must think they totally got away with it. So they'll see the NuAgra New Year's Eve party as a perfect chance to come after me again."

"That's not nearly as reassuring as you seem to think." Mom sends a beseeching glance at Dad. "Surely there's some safer way?"

He lifts a shoulder. "None we've thought of. We do have people digging into the records of all our newer arrivals. That may narrow the list of potential suspects, but it will take time. And that assumes whoever did this arrived during the most recent launch window. If it's an *Echtran* who's lived on Earth longer than that, I doubt there's any record at all of their political leanings."

"Mom, honestly, it'll be fine," I insist. "If M and I could locate Allister and Lennox all the way in Dun Cloch from here, and the freaking Grentl in *orbit*, we should have no problem pinpointing anyone twisted enough for murder if we're in the same room with them."

"If you're sure—?" Her worried frown eases slightly.

I nod vigorously. "I am. So is M. And it's not just about *my* safety. We'll *all* be safer once we've caught whoever this is."

Reluctantly, she nods. "Very well, though I can't say I like it. I do hope whatever you're planning works."

So do I.

The next day, our six person Bond Squad meets up in the arboretum again to sketch out a rough plan. First, though, the others want to know exactly what M and Molly told the Council last night about their *graell* bonds.

"As little as we could while sticking to the truth," Molly says. "We should all get our stories straight, though. Nara's already messaged me, wanting to know when she can have those Scientists run tests on Tristan and me. We wanted to talk to the rest of you before agreeing to anything."

"She messaged me, too," Kira says. "I put off answering because I wasn't sure how, um, public we want to go about us all having *graell* bonds. I mean, I haven't even told my parents yet."

"They'll probably react better than our mum did." Sean snorts and shakes his head. "Anyway, it's not like we can keep it secret for long, now the Council knows. But how much do we want to tell people about our, y'know, powers?"

Tristan and Molly exchange a glance. "We've talked about that," he says. "Seems like what Molly and I can do will become a lot less useful if everybody knows about it."

"Good point," M agrees. "The Council still doesn't know about the increased range of our telepathy, and I only told them last night about my emotion-sensing thing. Kyna and Mr. Stuart both think that should stay secret."

I nod. "Given the number of *Echtrans* who still have it in for us, it seems like a good idea to keep a few tricks up our sleeves. Probably true for your persuasive ability, too," I tell Molly and Tristan. "Maybe just let them test your electrical potential and telepathy? That should be enough to convince people you really are *graell* bonded, which is the important thing, right? Even more for Sean and Kira, being from different *fines*."

M and I have come in for plenty of criticism over that, since she's Royal—obviously—and I'm not. Because my dad is from the Informatics *fine* and my mom's a Healer, some *Echtrans* consider me a "half-breed," and therefore even *less* worthy of the Sovereign. At least Molly and Tristan are both Royals.

"You willing to go public about just that much?" Sean asks Kira.

Though clearly still reluctant, she nods. "Though I should probably give my family a heads-up first. I'd rather they not find out from some article in the *Echtran Enquirer*."

"Especially if Gwendolyn Gannett writes it." Molly grimaces. "Though now that M and I will be doing a weekly broadcast on the new *Echtran* News Network, we'll have another way to counter her crap, in addition to M's columns in the *Enquirer*. Maybe we should do a segment sometime soon about the *graell* and Shim's research proving it's real?"

M gives her an approving grin. "Good idea. Let's do that."

"So, back to the *slightly* more urgent matter of catching the person who tried to kill me," I say before the conversation goes completely off the rails. "The party is three days from now, right?"

"Right," Sean confirms. "New Year's Eve. Mum says they're expecting nearly three hundred *Echtrans* to attend, about the same number that came to the NuAgra dedication three weeks ago. Invites went out right after Thanksgiving and they started getting confirmations back right away."

Kira smiles. "I'm not surprised. Most of our people, especially the ones who don't work at NuAgra, are probably starved for more social interaction with other *Echtrans*. It gets…exhausting having to pretend all the time, worrying about making some slip in front of a *Duchas*."

"I remember," Molly says. "Though it gets easier. But that's good. The more people there, the better chance our assassin will be one of them."

"True," Tristan agrees. "So once the party starts, I guess we should deploy strategically around all the areas people will be to watch for anything suspicious?"

M looks at me and shrugs. "More or less," she says, "though that probably won't be necessary, since as soon as we get there, Rigel and I can start scanning. If anyone's planning an attack, we should be able to pick up on it pretty quickly. If we don't, we may ask you guys to help, um, boost us."

"What should we do once you identify the killer?" Kira asks. "Will the Council be okay with us taking them out right in the middle of their holiday party?"

"Hm, I hadn't thought about that." M frowns thoughtfully. "Though to be honest, I'm less worried about what the Council will think than the impression it would give everyone else there. We definitely don't want it to look like we're randomly targeting people for questioning, like some kind of police state. Assuming we can pinpoint the person, we should probably try to neutralize them quietly, away from the crowd. Otherwise we'll either have to explain the whole situation to everybody—kind of awkward at a party—or risk all kinds of rumors."

"Good point," Molly says. "The last thing we need is Gwendolyn Gannett concocting more conspiracy theories. Now that she'll have her own show, she's bound to do even more of the muckraking she does in her regular *Enquirer* gossip column."

We all fall silent for a moment.

Then Sean says, "How about once M and Rigel figure out who it is, we somehow herd the person away from the rest of the party— maybe into one of the greenhouses? Hey!" He looks at Kira. "Maybe you can do your 'Super Ag' thing and get some plant to spring up and immobilize them until Security comes."

Kira laughs. "Fun idea, but it doesn't work quite that fast. Not yet, anyway. Besides, all the plants there are edible, not the type that would grab someone, no matter how quickly they grow."

"Grapevines?" Sean suggests.

"Okay, there are a few vines," she admits. "Beans and melons and such. Or maybe we could make a pumpkin drop on his head. But we'd better not count on that as our main plan."

I chuckle along with the others. "The greenhouses might work as a place for a private takedown, but we should come up with a few other potential locations, just in case. There's no knowing where guests might decide to congregate."

"Molly and I can scope out likely places while we're at NuAgra on Tuesday to record our first show," M offers. "The less we have to improvise on the spot, the better the chance we can pull this off discreetly."

Since there's not much more we can plan for right now, M declares our little meeting over and the couples go their separate ways. M and I wander up Diamond Street, yet again scanning every *Echtran* we pass—which isn't many—for negative vibes. Nada.

"So," I say when we're almost to Dream Cream, "have you given any more thought to the Council's idea of you moving out to NuAgra until we catch this guy? Might not be a bad idea."

She frowns at me. "Not you, too? You do realize it would be almost impossible for us to get *any* private time together if I'm actually living there. Plus it would make it harder to do this kind of planning with the rest of the group. Anyway, you're the one the killer targeted. Maybe *you* should stay out there instead."

Startled, I laugh. "Doubt the Council would go for that—and I don't have quarters there, like you do."

"You can use mine," she offers, grinning.

Though I can tell she's mostly kidding, I shake my head. "I wouldn't be much of a Bodyguard if I agreed to that. How could I protect you from way out there?"

"You probably need protection more than I do right now," she says, wrinkling her nose in that cute way she has. "At least you have a car, so you wouldn't be totally trapped out there, like I would."

"Give it up, M. Not happening," I assure her. "I have a better idea. How about I stay as close to you as your aunt and uncle and my folks will let me, until this guy is caught? Then we can protect each other."

Squeezing my hand in hers, M smiles up at me. "Now *that's* a plan I can get behind!"

11

Face unafraid the plans that we've made

M

OVER THE NEXT THREE DAYS, Rigel and I do our best to follow our "stick close and protect each other" plan. Unfortunately, Aunt Theresa has other ideas. She always does a ton of baking—even more than usual—over the holidays, to donate to various local benefits. In the past, before she knew the truth about me, that meant I had to spend a whole lot of time in the kitchen. Even now I can tell she expects my help, though she's more polite about asking than in years past.

I'm positive telling her about the attempt on Rigel's life would scare her, so I mostly go along with it. Rigel comes over anyway, but it's obviously super boring for him to just sit in the kitchen while I help my aunt bake.

"Maybe your time would be better spent snooping around Glitterby's," I suggest after lunch Monday. "Do they have a security camera? Maybe it recorded someone messing with your package."

"No. I checked for that on Saturday," he tells me. "They don't even have wi-fi."

So much for that idea. "Who's researching the backgrounds of all the new arrivals?" I ask. "Maybe you can help with that?"

"Somebody up in Dun Cloch, my Dad said. So probably not. But if you're trying to get rid of me, I guess I can go home and find out for sure." He winks, knowing full well that's *not* what I'm doing. "You're still coming to dinner at our house tonight, right?"

"Absolutely. Meanwhile…be careful, okay?"

He promises, gives me a quick kiss and leaves. And I go back to measuring out flour and sugar.

Late that afternoon, my friend Bri calls. "Hey, M, are you and Rigel coming to the game tonight?"

"Game?" I echo, momentarily confused.

"Jewel's basketball game, duh!" She laughs. "Earth to M! I know you haven't been to that many this year, but Deb can't come tonight —she's helping with her mom's bookkeeping or something—and I don't want Liam to see me sitting by myself."

I'd totally forgotten there would be basketball games over winter break, even though I went to at least one of Sean's last year.

"Liam?" My antennae go up. "Does that mean you two are still, um, seeing each other?"

"Well…" She hesitates. "We haven't been on another date or anything, but he *did* invite me to come to his games."

Which she would have anyway. As he probably knew. I relax.

"Sorry, I can't tonight," I tell her. "I'm going over to Rigel's for dinner. Kira will probably be there, though. She goes to all of Sean's games unless she has one of her own."

"Yeah, I guess I can sit with her, then. Thanks, M." She hangs up and I take yet another sheet of cookies out of the oven.

Dinner at the Stuarts' is uneventful—which is nice. Especially since Dr. Stuart forbids any "business" talk over dinner, forcing us to stick with more general topics, like the holidays and school.

Rigel comes over again Tuesday morning, then drives Molly and me out to NuAgra to record our first joint, planet-wide talk show broadcast.

"You'll do great," he says when he drops us off. "I'm really looking forward to seeing it in a couple of days!"

As I give him a quick kiss goodbye, I try not to think about the fact that we're hoping to nab that assassin between now and then.

On entering the studio a few minutes later, I'm struck by how different it looks today. Instead of squashy chairs and floral prints, it's now furnished in a sleek, modern style, in muted shades of blue with silvery accents—just as Molly requested. I like it much better. Gwendolyn's set reminded me a little too strongly of Aunt Theresa's old-fashioned decor.

The recording session itself goes surprisingly smoothly, almost exactly as Molly and I rehearsed it Sunday night. Though later on we plan to interview various people from our brand-new, expanded *Echtran* government, we decided against guests for our initial episode. Instead, we take turns informally interviewing each other in hopes we'll seem friendly and approachable to our *Echtran* viewers —real people they can trust, rather than figureheads with fancy titles.

By our third take, we're both relaxed enough to inject a little humor as we answer each other's questions, even teasing each other occasionally—like the sisters we are. We had already become close friends before discovering our blood relationship two months ago. Now it's hard to believe we didn't instinctively realize it sooner.

After we finish and Carleen declares the recording usable, Molly and I spend an hour or so wandering around NuAgra. We pretend we're just getting to know the place better, since even if we don't move in anytime soon, we'll be expected to spend more and more time here. In reality, we're taking note of every out-of-the-way room, hallway or corner where our Bond Squad might reasonably corral an assassin tomorrow night.

"One of these greenhouses still might be our best bet," Molly says when we make it to the rear of the complex. "But now we have a few other options. Assuming the person we're after actually shows up."

"If not, we'll go to plan B," I say with more confidence than I feel.

Molly raises a skeptical brow. "Do we have a plan B?"

Shrugging, I grin at her. "Not yet, but I'm sure we'll come up with something. We didn't have a plan for Devyn and his Ossian Sphere, but we handled that pretty well. Anyway, odds are they'll show. Especially after Gwendolyn Gannett's bit in today's *Echtran Enquirer*."

As Molly suggested, Kyna "accidentally" sent her the list of those expected to attend, including us, Rigel, Tristan, Sean and Kira. I can't imagine anyone upset enough about Rigel and me—and maybe Sean and Kira?—to attempt murder will be able to stay away.

By the following evening, nothing else suspicious has occurred, but that also means we have no new leads. As agreed, our Bond Squad hangs out in the NuAgra parking lot in the O'Garas' minivan until the New Years Eve party is underway. This was my idea—I reasoned that the whole group of us making an entrance might spark an emotional reaction in the killer, making them that much easier to pinpoint.

Two security guards are stationed just outside the main entry door, electronically scanning each guest before they palm themselves inside. Mr. Stuart insisted on that, even though he admitted those scans can't detect toxins. At least no one will be able to sneak in a bomb or an energy weapon.

As the six of us approach, the guards snap to attention, then bow deeply.

"Welcome, Excellencies," the older of the two greets us. "All should be secure inside, but we and four others stand ready to assist if necessary."

We thank them, submit to a cursory scan, then pass through the doors to the lavishly decorated reception hall.

For a moment, all I can do is stare. Above the milling throng, silver stars sparkle and gold streamers gently undulate, throwing off iridescent glints with each movement. A holographic illusion, I belatedly realize, but beautiful—and impressive. Instrumental holiday music plays softly in the background, complementing the scene.

"Wow," Kira breathes from just behind me.

"Pretty," Sean agrees. "But I guess we should get to work, huh?"

Nodding, my hand firmly in Rigel's, I move forward, sharpening my focus as we progress into the room. As we're spotted by the nearest guests, they bow to Molly and me, alerting others to our presence. Within moments, most eyes in the hall are on us.

Smiling around at the assemblage, Rigel and I keep walking as I widen my emotion-sensing to take in the whole, huge room. Molly and Tristan pace us to my left, Sean and Kira to Rigel's right. Soon, people begin tentatively coming up to Molly and me to wish us happy holidays. As we respond to each person, I pull in my focus again to gauge their emotions.

The first few are as expected—admiring and a bit awed by meeting their Sovereign and her sister. Briefly scanning wide again, I do pick up a few scattered clusters of negativity. Also expected, since polls suggest more than a quarter of *Echtrans* still disapprove of my relationship with Rigel. Nothing I'm sensing seems hostile enough to indicate a potential murderer, though. What if they don't come tonight after all? That would put us back at square one.

Narrowing my probing to individuals again, I make my way toward the denser crowd at the center of the room, where the main reception desk has been converted into a big, U-shaped table holding a lavish spread of food and drinks. The O'Garas and a few other Council members are there, including Kyna. I'm surprised to see her, since I'd thought she couldn't attend, but when I get close I realize she's just here holographically.

Not so Nara, who comes forward eagerly.

"Ah, here you are," she exclaims. "I was hoping for a word with you all this evening, especially Princess Malena and Sean and their new bond-mates. Have you had time to discuss my requests?"

"Er…" Sean glances at Kira, then me. "Yes. We're willing to talk to those Scientists about what's, um, happened. Sometime."

Molly and Tristan both nod. "Not tonight, though," Molly hastens to add in response to Nara's delighted smile.

"No, no, of course not," Nara replies, still beaming. "But perhaps this weekend, before your school is back in session?"

As they all agree to that, I turn to Rigel's dad.

"Is everyone here who said they'd be? Do you know?"

"Not quite," he replies, glancing down at the tablet in his hand.

"I've been keeping tabs as security checks people in. I take it you haven't—?"

Rigel shakes his head. "Not yet, but we only just got here. We'll keep looking. I can ping your omni if we spot any likely suspects."

"Please do. I have a team standing by…discreetly." Mr. Stuart nods toward a hallway on our right that leads to NuAgra's government complex.

Leaving the refreshment area, we separate into couples so Kira and Tristan, both with Bodyguard training, can peek into some of the adjoining rooms to see if there are partygoers in other areas. Meanwhile, Rigel and I continue our casual-seeming circuit of the room while I probe the emotions of each individual we pass or speak with.

Our linked hands provoke occasional frowns accompanied by varying degrees of distaste, though nothing I'd call sinister. Several minutes later we've made our way to the rear doors that lead out to the greenhouses, where the other two couples rejoin us.

"So far, everyone seems to be in this area, probably because that's where the food is," Sean tells us. "I don't blame them, it smells great."

"No luck spotting our perp yet?" Tristan asks.

I shake my head. "Let's head back toward the refreshment table. Nara kept me from focusing properly there before. And the crowd around it keeps shifting."

We're nearly back to the central hub of the room when I nearly stumble, I'm so startled by an intense wave of hatred from somewhere off to my left.

Because we're touching, Rigel immediately picks it up, too. *That's got to be him, right?* The others, oblivious, keep walking.

Must be, I think back, forcing myself to move forward again as I glance that way, surreptitiously probing everyone in the vicinity of that overwhelmingly negative vibe. I see six people standing a little apart from the others who all look less than happy. Narrowing my focus, I sense strong irritation from five of them. However the sixth, a woman, broadcasts a truly murderous hostility.

The tall, dark one? Rigel silently asks.

Definitely, I send back. *The last time I felt vibes this awful were from that assassin who tried to kill Molly last month.*

I realize it's going to be tricky to extricate our target from the crowd, especially her group of apparent friends, without alarming everyone else at the party.

By now, the other four members of our "Squad" have back-tracked to us, all looking concerned.

"Hey," Molly whispers. "Have you—?"

"We think so," I murmur back, "but we all need to play it cool if we don't want to spook her into panicking."

Donning a smile, I approach the group. "Thank you for coming tonight," I say cheerfully. "Are you having a nice time?"

Though clearly startled, they all manage to smile back—even the one sending out waves of hatred.

"Yes, Excellency, thank you," one of the other women responds. "I'm Honoria and this is my husband, Starn, Mechanics *fine.*"

They both bow to Molly and me, then the others speak up, intro-ducing themselves as Vernon and Sharra, and Fergus and Noreen—the hostile one. Those four are also Mechanics, generally considered one of the "lower" *fines* back in Nuath, along with Maintenance and Waste Management.

As I exchange a few polite nothings with them, I delve more deeply into each one's emotions. Other than Noreen, their disap-proval seems aimed almost exclusively at Rigel, with far more posi-tive feelings toward Molly and me. Noreen, on the other hand, is barely concealing something close to fury.

"It's an honor to finally meet you in person, Excellency." Noreen's smile is distinctly at odds with her intensely negative emotions. "There were so many things I wanted to ask about, but…I can't help feeling a bit flustered. Would you mind terribly if I talk with your non-Royal friends, instead?" She nods toward Rigel and Kira. "I find them a bit less, ah, intimidating."

She's planning something, I think to Rigel, alarmed.

Probably, but it gives us a chance to get her by herself. We need that, right?

Ideally, yes, but I don't like it. Do NOT let her touch you!

Rigel takes a casual half-step back, his smile still firmly in place. "We'd be happy to answer any questions you have, Noreen. We can talk over here, where it's a little quieter, if you'd like." He motions to an open archway just a few feet away—the same hallway his dad indicated earlier.

"Perfect!" Her smile widens and now I sense a fierce excitement along with her hatred of Rigel. And Kira?

Under the circumstances, I'm super reluctant to let go of Rigel's hand—but I also want to avoid a scene if possible. *Stay where I can see you, okay? I'll listen in from here.*

With a tiny nod, Rigel releases my hand to follow the woman. Kira goes with him, hiding the nervousness I sense from her admirably. Though he doesn't attempt to intervene, Sean shoots me a look every bit as worried as I feel.

I fervently hope we won't both regret this.

12

Catch me if you can

Rigel

I MAKE sure Kira doesn't get any closer to this Noreen woman than I do as we accompany her away from the main party area. From what I sensed through M, this nut job hates Kira nearly as much as me—though not quite. Because she also threatens the "purity" of the Royal bloodline? Probably. I don't get why a non-Royal would even care about that, but I've learned a lot of them do.

When we're far enough away from the crowd for our conversation to be masked by the holiday music, Noreen turns to face us both.

"I can't tell you how much I appreciate this opportunity." Her smile takes on a more sinister quality. "It's perfect, really. And just when I thought I'd lost my one chance to make things right."

"What things?" I reach into my pocket to ping my dad's omni as promised, while keeping my line of communication with M wide open.

Noreen's smile becomes almost feral. "Between our Sovereign and her rightful Consort, of course. The two of you have disrupted not only the natural order, but what *should* have been the romance of the century! Back in Nuath, I watched every feed they were in together. It was clear to everyone how very much in love they were. Are."

As she talks, Kira and I both edge sideways until the hallway is behind us and Noreen's back is to the big reception hall. She goes along with it, probably thinking she has us trapped now. But over her shoulder, I see M and the others moving silently our way. Where are Dad's security guys?

"I don't know what you did to our Sovereign to lure her back into the disgusting dalliance you had with her last year," Noreen continues, openly glaring at me now, "but someone clearly needs to free her from your influence. Since no one else has stepped up, as a true patriot, I mean to do it myself."

On those words, she slips both hands into small, nearly-invisible pockets on either side of her long skirt.

Without hesitation, Kira spins around and aims a high kick to the woman's head. She ducks surprisingly quickly, so it only grazes her. Though she goes down on one knee, she springs right back up. Then, dark eyes blazing, she launches herself toward us. Each outstretched hand now holds a tiny ampule like the ones we found embedded in the beignet bag.

Before she can touch either one of us, I grab her right wrist. Kira makes a grab for her left, but the woman jerks her arm back just in time.

"Oh, no you don't," she snarls. "I read you both have Body-guard training, so I took a little something on my way here to give me a quick boost. It only needs to last long enough for me to—" She darts forward again, her free hand aiming directly for Kira's forearm.

When Kira dances back, the woman shifts her focus to me, jabbing the ampule at my hand that's holding her wrist. I'm forced to let go to avoid being stuck and instantly killed. But that gives Noreen the use of both hands again.

Did she touch you? M thinks to me in alarm.

The others are right behind the would-be killer now, but with the way she's waving those two ampules around, they don't dare just grab her.

Not quite. But it's going to be tricky to stop her without getting stuck. What happened to the security guys?

I contacted your dad, M tells me. *I was afraid his team might spook her into killing either herself or someone else.*

"Ma'am? You don't really want to do this, do you?" Molly suddenly calls out in her most persuasive voice.

Startled, Noreen swings around to find the rest of our group blocking the entrance to the hallway. "Absolutely, I do!" she tells Molly, apparently too crazed to be affected by her power. "Dispatching this interloper so our Sovereign and her true love can be together again will finally give my life meaning. I'll be a hero to thousands!"

While she's distracted, I try to get hold of Noreen's wrist again but she jumps away from me, now brandishing the ampules at anyone who tries to get close.

In case you hadn't noticed, I think to M, *this woman is completely bonkers. No reasoning with her.*

Let me try— Breaking off her thought to me, M forcefully says, "Stop! Drop those!"

The strength of her "push" paralyzes even me for a second. Unfortunately, Noreen is either too unhinged or too amped up on whatever she took to be similarly affected.

Instead, she takes advantage of my temporary immobility to spring to my side—just as three security guys come barreling out of a nearby doorway.

"One more step and he's dead!" Noreen screams.

The security team freezes, looking to M for guidance. Behind her in the reception hall, I see my dad racing this way. I'm no longer paralyzed, but don't dare move with both ampules poised less than an inch from my throat.

Kira is off to the side looking nearly as frustrated as I feel. I catch her eye.

"Get back to Sean," I tell her. "At least she won't get both of us."

Noreen lets out a wild, insane laugh. "Yes, run away, girlie.

Taking you out would have been a nice bonus, but I'm sure once this...*abomination* is out of the way—" the ampules move closer— "the Royal Consort will drop you as the plaything you are to reunite with our Sovereign. Then everything will again be as it should be."

At my nod, Kira rushes over to Sean, who immediately puts an arm around her.

"Please," Molly tries again, her ability reinforced by Tristan's hand around hers. "You don't have to do this. Why don't you tell us exactly what it is you want?"

"I want this vile seducer *dead*, that's what I want," Noreen snaps at her. "It's the only way our dear Sovereign Emileia will feel completely free to love Sean O'Gara again. He—"

She breaks off with a gasp as both ampules suddenly fly up into the air, high above her head.

"What—? How—?"

Noreen tries to leap after the floating vials but I swiftly catch hold of her arms and yank them behind her. The security team now springs into action, taking over from me to secure her wrists with unbreakable ties. As the ampules slowly drift to the floor, well away from everyone, my dad and Noreen's friends all converge at the hall-way's entrance.

"Unhand my wife!" the largest man, Fergus shouts. "This is an outrage!"

"Outrage?" my dad snarls back. "Your wife tried to kill my son— twice. And murdered an innocent *Duchas* woman in the process."

Fergus turns baffled eyes on the bound woman. "Noreen? What is he saying? That can't be true. Can it?"

"What if it is?" She glares defiantly back. "You've said yourself that someone should get rid of this filth." She spits the word at me. "I saw an opportunity, so I took it. That stupid *Duchas* only got what she deserved for spoiling my beautiful plan."

Clearly aghast, Fergus stares at her for a long moment. Then, drawing himself up to his full height, he turns to my dad. "Your boy there looks fine to me. Whatever my wife tried to do, she obviously failed. You can't possibly arrest her for accidentally killing some stupid *Duchas*."

"Yes, we certainly can," Dad coldly responds. "For both that and the attempted murder of my son."

"And Kira," I chime in. "She tried to kill her just now, too."

I turn to the security guys. "Search her, in case she has more of those things—but be really careful. The smallest prick from one could be fatal."

Nodding, two men hustle her away.

A moment later, Mr. and Mrs. O'Gara hurry up. "I understand I'm needed to question someone?" Mrs. O asks.

Dad nods. "She's in room seven, but keep your distance until she's been thoroughly searched."

Fergus and the other two couples now begin hastily backing away, but at a nod from Dad, the remaining security guard moves to block their retreat.

"We'll want all of you to answer a few questions as well," Dad tells them. "Take them to room six."

Though they all look rebellious, they go with the guard without protest. Both O'Garas follow them down the hallway.

Dad sweeps a concerned glance over me, then the rest of us. "Are you sure you're all right? I should oversee the questioning."

"I'm fine, Dad," I assure him. "We all are—thanks to Sean and Kira." I send them a grateful look, then point at the ampules on the floor. "Make sure someone safely disposes of those ASAP."

"Will do," Dad says. "Meanwhile, you should all rejoin the party before too many people begin asking questions."

13

Merry and bright

M

MY HEART IS STILL HAMMERING as Rigel finishes talking to his dad and heads my way. The instant he's within reach, I throw my arms around him, not caring who might be watching. I can't believe how close I came to losing him—*again*!

"I'm fine, M. Really," Rigel reassures me, picking up on my thought.

"I...I know." By degrees, I start to relax. His touch always has that effect on me. "But I felt so *helpless*. I was dying to take her out with a lightning bolt, but I can't do that without you, and—"

He stops my emotional babbling with a kiss. "I'm sorry I didn't handle things better, keep you from going through that. But at least now, with Mrs. O'Gara's help, Dad's security people can find out if there are any other immediate threats nearby."

Taking a deep breath, I nod. "Yes. That's good. Though if Noreen's husband wasn't in on the plot, I doubt the others were, either. She's the only one I sensed as being that crazy hostile."

Molly overhears me and frowns. "Do you think that's why I couldn't convince her to stop and listen? Because she's, y'know, crazy?"

"That, plus she apparently took something, some drug, to temporarily make her faster and stronger," Rigel says. "She told us so. Maybe it also made her more resistant to your persuasion?"

I blink. "Huh. That must be why my 'push' command didn't work on her, either. I didn't even think about it making *you* stop," I tell Rigel apologetically. "Instead of helping, I nearly got you killed!"

He puts a comforting arm around my shoulders. "How could you possibly know it wouldn't work on her? Even without that drug, as obsessed as she was, there probably wasn't room in her brain for anything but getting rid of me. Really glad she's in custody now."

"So am I." Relief surges through me again as I smile up at him. "I've spent the whole past week trying to hide how worried I was about you."

"Yeah, I could tell," he admits. "But if you knew I knew, you'd have worried about that, too. So I didn't let on."

As we reach the center of the big lobby area, Council member Breann approaches us. "Has the, ah, matter been taken care of?" She glances over my shoulder.

I nod. "Mr. Stuart and his security team have the assassin and her friends in a holding room. Mrs. O'Gara is helping to question them now."

"Oh, good." She smiles. "Kyna wanted me to ask you to say a few words to our guests shortly before midnight—if you're willing? I'm sure they'd all appreciate it."

"Oh! Um, sure, I guess so." I should have expected this, since I'm frequently called on to give little speeches whenever there's a signifi-cant gathering of *Echtrans*. "Just let me know when."

She promises to do that and our group moves on to the refresh-ment table. All six of us were too keyed up earlier to eat or drink anything, and I suddenly realize I'm starving. The others are, too, judging by how much food they heap onto their plates. For the next twenty minutes, we're too busy eating to discuss what happened—which we shouldn't do in public, anyway.

Everything is delicious. Those new food recombinators must have been working overtime this evening. I'm just finishing an amazing confection of chocolate and whipped cream when dance music starts playing from the hidden speakers around the reception hall.

"You know," Rigel says, "even though it wasn't exactly my fault, it *was* because of me that your holidays have been so stressful. I'd like to make that up to you, if I can."

By now, the last vestiges of my earlier terror for Rigel have dissipated, leaving me almost giddy. "You can start by asking me to dance," I playfully tell him.

In response, Rigel gives me an exaggerated bow. "Excellency, would you care to dance?"

I giggle, then punch his arm. "Haven't I told you not to call me that? But yes, I'd love to."

Turning, I see that most of the back half of the reception hall has magically become a dance floor. The tiles in that area, usually a cool blue-gray, now swirl with red, green and gold sparkles. Another holographic effect, I assume, or maybe the tiles are like the reactive glass I saw in Nuath, and actually change colors.

Already, a few couples are drifting onto it. Molly and Tristan also head that way, as do Sean and Kira. Rigel and I are following the other two couples when I see the Walsh twins, Liam and Lucas, standing off to the side. Still in a playful mood, I angle their way.

"I guess you guys didn't manage to scare up dates for tonight?" I ask teasingly.

Lucas smiles, shrugs and shakes his head, but Liam looks a little disgruntled by my question, making me immediately regret asking.

"Don't worry," I tell him. "More *Echtran* girls our age are sure to arrive during the next launch window, though I know a year and a half is a long time to wait. You, um, looked like you had a good time at Jewel's Winter Formal, at least."

He smiles then, more widely than his brother. "I did. I had a great time! Wish I could have invited Bri to this." He gazes around the beautifully decorated reception hall. "She'd love it."

The wistful quality in those last words prompts me to probe his feelings before Rigel can remind me again that it's none of my business. What I sense startles me.

"You really like Bri, don't you?"

His eyes, now wary, snap back to me. "Yeah. Yeah, I do. It's too bad— Well, you know. At least I get to see her at all my games. There's nothing wrong with that, right?"

"No, of course not," I quickly reassure him, at the same time making a mental note to attend the next basketball game myself. If he and Bri are actually starting to fall for each other—

Rigel gently tugs my arm, interrupting that thought. "C'mon, let's dance," he says with a wink.

With a parting smile at the Walsh twins, I willingly go with him.

You were doing it again, he silently chides me. *Didn't you agree to save your emotion-sensing for important stuff?*

I know, I think back. *I shouldn't have invaded Liam's privacy like that. I'll…try not to do it again. It's just that if Bri—*

Again, he stops me with a quick kiss. "Let's dance," he repeats, putting both arms around me.

I slide my hands up to his shoulders and we begin swaying to the strains of Nat King Cole's "Christmas Song"—one of my favorites.

You know, even death threats haven't kept this holiday season from being massively better than our last one, he thinks to me.

Remembering the awkwardness of the previous New Year's Eve, where we both had to pretend I was dating Sean during a party at the Stuarts' house, I can't disagree.

At a quarter to midnight, Breann motions me over to the refreshment table, now covered with tall glasses filled with sparkling liquid. I wonder if it's Champagne or *Spakriga*, the Nuathan equivalent. Either way, I won't be partaking.

Just in front of the central table, a small platform rises out of the floor. I see the O'Garas and Rigel's parents speaking together nearby, so I detour slightly to talk to them.

"How did the questioning go?" I ask quietly. "What did you find out?"

"That Noreen woman was apparently acting alone," Mr. Stuart tells me. "The others claimed to have no knowledge of her plans. Lili confirmed they were telling the truth."

She nods. "They did all confess—rather reluctantly—that in principle they agree with her that you would be better off with Sean. But only Noreen became obsessed to the extreme of attempting to kill anyone. She admitted—and her husband confirmed—that in recent weeks she has spent most of her time re-watching recordings of the two of you, from your time in Nuath. I recall some of those video feeds did rather, ah, romanticize your apparent relationship with my son. I'm afraid Noreen bought completely into that fantasy, to the point she was unable to separate it from reality."

I refrain from pointing out that Mrs. O herself worked pretty hard to make that same fantasy come true. Not that it did any good. No political arguments could ever have broken my bond with Rigel, or diminished my love for him.

"So her radicalization had nothing to do with Devyn Kane?" Rigel asks from just behind me.

His father shakes his head. "It seems not, beyond giving too much credence to some of the propaganda his adherents have been spreading. She must have obtained the toxin from one of them. Unfortunately, even though Devyn himself has now gone deep into hiding, the ideas he sparked are still circulating among some of our people."

"Molly and I will do our best to counter that in our weekly broadcast," I promise. "And I'll keep writing my columns for the *Enquirer*."

"Excellency, it's time," Breann whispers at my elbow.

I take the tiny microphone button she hands me and affix it to the neckline of my sparkly green holiday dress. Stepping up onto the little stage, I touch the button and clear my throat. The sound echoes through the enormous room and the boisterous chatter immediately dies down.

"Thank you for coming tonight, everyone," my voice booms out from the speakers. "I know this has been a somewhat stressful year for those of you who volunteered to leave your homes in Nuath to come to Earth, for the good of our colony there. I'd like to again express my appreciation for that sacrifice, and for the efforts you've been making to assimilate into Earth society.

"Adapting to a new planet and culture is no easy thing, I know, but by all reports, most of you are doing an admirable job of it so far. As we move into a bright new year, both on Earth and in Nuath, I have no doubt that progress will continue. In fact, I hope that this coming year will prove one of the best ever in *Echtran* and Nuathan history. With your help, I promise to do all I can to turn that hope into reality. Happy New Year, everyone!"

As I step off the dais, the final one-minute countdown to midnight begins.

Hastily, everyone who isn't already holding one arms themselves with a filled glass, to drink the traditional toast—a tradition I'm told is also common on Mars. A woman approaches Rigel and me with a tray of tall glasses. I start to wave her away when Mr. O'Gara steps forward.

"Not to worry, Excellency, we made a point of providing non-inebriating *Spakriga* for our younger guests. That's what this is."

Relieved—my experience with real *Spakriga* back in Nuath was an unpleasant one—I take a glass, as does Rigel.

"Five!" I hear people in the crowd shout out in response to the enormous gold numerals that have appeared in midair over my head. "Four! Three! Two! One! Happy New Year!"

Glittering, holographic confetti begins falling to the strains of "Auld Lang Syne."

Rigel clinks his glass against mine. "Here's to *our* best year ever," he murmurs.

The love in his hazel eyes as he holds my gaze fills me with joy. We drink, then he gathers me into his arms for a New Year's kiss.

"I love you, Rigel," I whisper against his lips. "For this year and for always."

Though his lips are now too delightfully busy to answer aloud, he responds directly to my mind.

Ditto. For always. Happy New Year, M.

The End

Keep reading for a sneak peek at **Unraveling the Stars**, the next book in the Starstruck Series!

Unraveling the Stars (preview)

Deb

GLANCING at the clock on the gym wall, I frown. The Winter Formal is nearly half over, and I've barely made any progress toward getting to know my date better.

"Did you go to many dances at your old school?" I ask him as the current song ends.

Lucas, the guy I've been crushing on since the day he arrived at Jewel High three months ago, shakes his head. "Not really, no."

"This must be your first one here?" I persist, determined to draw him out at least a little.

"Um, yeah, I heard we just missed Jewel High's Homecoming." It's the longest sentence he's said to me so far.

I nod. "That's right. It was the very weekend before you all started school here. It looks like all of you have settled in pretty well by now, though?"

"I think so. My brother's definitely enjoying it here."

We both turn to look at Liam, Lucas's identical twin, who's

laughing over something with my best friend, Bri, a short distance away.

"It definitely shows on the basketball court," I comment, grinning.

Bri, who goes to all the games, claims Liam's nearly as good a player as Sean O'Gara, who took Jewel to State in basketball last year.

"Yeah. It definitely does." There's an edge to Lucas's words that makes me glance up in time to see him smoothing a frown.

Before I can think how to ask him about it, the next song starts, too loud to talk over while dancing.

Is he jealous of how well his brother plays? Seems unlikely, when Lucas never even tried out for the team, or acts like he's into sports at all. Liam, on the other hand, is as bit a sports nut as Bri—which is why she was more interested in him from the start. When he asked her to tonight's dance, she was at least as thrilled as I was when Lucas asked me—though maybe not as astonished.

I sneak another peek up at Lucas, surreptitiously admiring his strong profile, perfectly disordered dark brown hair and gray-blue eyes. Again.

From their first day at Jewel, a month into the fall semester, I was much more drawn to Lucas than Liam, even though I met Liam first. The brothers are equally gorgeous, of course, and outgoing Liam *is* easier to talk to. But I sensed a quiet strength in shy Lucas, along with a certain vulnerability that captivated me from the moment I introduced myself in Art, the one class we have together.

Over the next three months, I tried multiple times to engage Lucas in conversation before, during and after class. but never made much headway. Since he hardly talked to anybody, I didn't take it personally—or let it keep me from obsessing over him. Honestly, though, I wasn't completely sure Lucas even knew my name until three days ago when, totally out of the blue, he invited me to this dance. Needless to say, I was over the moon!

Earlier this evening, when Bri and I were getting ready for the dance together, we couldn't stop talking about our luck in snagging the gorgeous Walsh twins as dates.

"Y'know, Deb," Bri said while smoothing her hair with a new pomade she just bought, "if we play our cards right, tonight might be the start of two beautiful romances."

"Wouldn't that be wonderful?" I sighed. "Hey, can I try some of that stuff?"

Bri handed me the jar with a shrug. I knew the product was intended for "Black" hair, which Bri's sort of is, but I hoped it might also tame my blonde, flyaway frizz. It helped some. By the time the boys picked us up for the dance at Bri's house, we both agreed we looked the best we ever had.

"Do you want to get something to drink?" I ask Lucas when yet another loud, fast dance song begins.

"Oh, um, sure," he agrees.

Together, we head toward the folded-up bleachers, where a long table holds big dispensers of water and lemonade. As we cross the school gym, I notice how he has to duck to avoid hitting a few of the lowest-hanging paper snowflakes. I don't, of course. I'm probably the shortest girl in the junior class, while Lucas is one of the taller guys—taller than M's boyfriend, Rigel, if not quite as tall as Sean.

"What was your last school like?" I ask as he hands me a paper cup of lemonade. "Bigger than Jewel, I'll bet."

"A little bigger, yeah."

When he doesn't elaborate, I try again. "Where was it exactly? Somewhere in upstate New York?" I remember Liam mentioning that in Pre-Cal class once.

Lucas nods. "Between Syracuse and Utica."

"Is that where NuAgra's headquarters used to be before Jewel?"

He flashes me an uncertain look. "Um, yeah. Though it wasn't as big as the one they built here."

"So NuAgra is expanding? Does that mean they're making progress on developing those superior crops I read they're working on? That'll be good, won't it?"

He nods again. "I think so."

"Is that what your parents do out there? Work with the new plant strains? Are they, like, botanists?"

"No, engineers. They work with the, uh, mechanical systems there."

He still looks wary, though I don't know why. I'm asking perfectly normal questions.

"Engineers? That's interesting. Is that what you want to go to college for, after high school? I remember Liam saying you're in AP Calculus, so you must be really good in math."

"Er…yeah, I guess."

Because he seems so uncomfortable, I blurt out, "Sorry. I know I'm asking a lot of questions. It's not that I'm nosy, I'm just trying to break the ice."

"Ice?" His brows go up, like he's totally confused…which confuses me. "What ice?"

I blink. "You know. Break the ice. Start a conversation."

"Oh. Right. Of course." He's clearly covering "It's, um, fine."

Can he really never have heard that expression before? I'm suddenly reminded of another time, when I tried to flirt with him in Art class by saying, "Penny for your thoughts." He was confused then, too, so I had to explain what *that* phrase meant. Weird.

A moment later we finish our lemonade and head back to the dance floor….just in time for a slow dance. My heart speeds up as I try to hide my nervousness.

During our first two slow dances, Lucas was a perfect gentleman, his hands never straying so much as a fraction of an inch from where they rested lightly on my shoulder blades. Totally unlike my Homecoming date, who used the slow numbers to push the limits as far as I'd let him—which wasn't very far.

Like all the others, he quickly lost interest when he discovered Bri and M's "cute little friend" wasn't as easy as he'd hoped. I'm relieved Lucas isn't like that but, okay, also a tiny bit disappointed that he hasn't even *tried*. Yet?

This time, when I put my hands on his shoulders, I move a tiny bit closer than before, though not quite touching anywhere else. Just to see…

But though a hint of a smile suggests he noticed, Lucas doesn't take advantage, again keeping me at a perfectly respectful distance through the whole song.

Darn it.

It's looking like that goodnight kiss I've dreamed about since he asked me to the dance won't happen after all. Still, I feel like Lucas and I *might* be establishing the beginnings of what might at least become a beautiful friendship. And maybe more, eventually?

A few songs later, I notice M, Molly and Bri all heading toward the ladies' room. Eager for a chance to compare notes about our evening, I politely excuse myself to Lucas to follow them. The other three girls don't see me, so they go into the restroom before I can catch up. When I push open the door a second later, I can hear Bri already talking to the others.

"—really glad Lucas followed through and asked Deb. When I told Liam I'd only come to the dance with him if his brother went with Deb, I was terrified he'd tell me to forget it. Which would have been *awful*, because I'm having a super great time with him tonight! Luckily he did talk Lucas into asking her—and the two of them seem to be having fun together. Oh! But don't either of you *dare* tell Deb I told you that! She'd be totally mortified."

M and Molly promise not to say a word as I freeze, then back up to let the door swing silently shut in front of my face. For a second I just stand there. Then, my throat suddenly tight, I turn and head for a different bathroom, the next hall over.

So *that's* why Lucas has been so meticulously polite all evening! Asking me to the Winter Formal was never his idea at all, just a favor he did for his brother and Bri. I wonder how hard Liam had to work to persuade him…?

The farther restroom is blessedly empty. I linger there until I'm sure I'm not going to cry, scolding myself for being so sensitive.

After all, Bri and I *did* ask Kira to put in a good word for us with the two Walsh brothers, I remind myself. It wasn't the first time we'd begged a friend to help us snag dates, either. Plenty of girls do that all the time. How is this any different?

Somehow, though, it is. Maybe because I've never before cared so much whether a boy liked me or not.

Once Lucas arrived at Jewel High, Art quickly became the class I looked forward to most—because of him. We'd barely exchanged a handful of words before I started weaving all kinds of romantic fantasies. When I caught him looking my way once or twice, I pretended it meant he was attracted to me, too, just too shy to do anything about it. So I thought when he asked me to tonight's dance, it proved I was right, that my dreams really could come true.

Now my foolish dreams feel more like a humiliating nightmare.

Tempting as it is to hide in the bathroom until the end of the dance, it's not really a viable option. Besides, I refuse to be *that* lame and cowardly! So, after a few deep breaths to steady myself, I make my way back to the gym. There, I pause outside the open double doors for one more fortifying breath before going in to rejoin my date.

"Sorry I was gone so long," I breathlessly apologize when I reach him. "I, um, got to talking." To myself, anyway.

Rather to my surprise, Lucas's gray-blue eyes show concern. "You're okay, then? Nothing's wrong?"

"Wrong?" I try for a little laugh but it sounds brittle to my ears. "Of course not. Oh, I like this song. C'mon."

Turning away from his too-perceptive gaze, I move toward the dance floor. To my relief, he follows without probing any further.

And why would he? Even if he can tell I'm upset, there's no particular reason it should matter to him. It's not like this is a *real* date, with a girl he actually wanted to be with.

By the end of the Formal half an hour later, I've mostly overcome my disappointment. I even maintain a relatively cheerful front when Lucas again avoids touching me more than absolutely necessary during the final dance, a slow one. I keep my distance, too, embarrassed now to think how close I got to him earlier. It must have made him super uncomfortable.

When the music finally stops, Lucas surprises me with a genuine-seeming smile that makes him heart-stoppingly handsome. "Thanks for coming with me tonight, Deb. It's been fun."

I smile back. "It has." And it was...until half an hour ago. "Thanks for asking me. I, um, guess we should go find Bri and your brother, huh?"

After the four of us retrieve our coats from our lockers, we head to the parking lot, Bri and Liam continuing their earlier conversation about—what else?—sports.

"It's practically a crime that you've never had a chance to attend an NBA game in person," Bri is telling him. "If my dad can score tickets to a Pacers game this season, I'll ask him to get one for you, too. For all of you, if you want," she adds, belatedly including Lucas and me.

Lucas shrugs at exactly the same time I do. "Don't go to any trouble on my account," he says.

"Or mine." I'd hate to be a third wheel all the way to Indy and back with Bri and Liam, even if I did care about pro basketball. Which I don't.

Despite that brief moment of unity, the drive home is awkward. Liam is driving, so Bri sits up front with him while Lucas and I are in back. I'm careful to stay well on my side of the seat.

When we reach Bri's house, I immediately jump out of the car so Lucas won't feel like he has to walk me to the door. Bri, on the other hand, is pretty obviously angling for a goodnight kiss, so waits for Liam to come around and open her door. That means Lucas has to get out of the car, too, or look rude—which he wouldn't want to do.

"It's kind of late," Bri says when we reach her front porch, "but do you guys want to come in for a few minutes?"

"Sure, if you—" Liam starts to say when his brother gives him a tiny head-shake that I probably wasn't supposed to see. "Uh, actually, I guess we'd better not. Our parents will expect us back."

Bri's disappointment is embarrassingly evident. "Oh, okay. I guess we'll, um, see you after the holidays, then."

"Unless you want to come to Monday night's game?" Liam suggests. "We also have two others scheduled over the break."

I'm pretty sure I'm the only one who notices how Lucas tenses as

Bri enthusiastically agrees, happy enough now that she hardly pouts at all when the boys head back to their parents' car.

"Oh, well. No goodnight kisses, but at least we'll get to see them again before school starts back up," she says as they drive off. "Did you have as much fun tonight as I did? You looked like you did. Aren't they both so dreamy?"

"Yeah, they are," I have to agree. "And yeah, I mostly did. Have a good time, I mean."

She quirks a dark eyebrow at me. "Only mostly? C'mon, you've been mooning over Lucas Walsh for three months. Didn't he live up to your expectations?"

I just shrug.

"Okay, what did he do wrong?" she presses. "You weren't expecting a marriage proposal on your first date, were you?"

At that, my intention to keep my humiliation to myself evaporates. "Hardly. Especially considering you *forced* Liam to make him ask me to the dance," I snap.

Her brown eyes go wide and startled. "How did you— I mean— It wasn't…"

"I overheard what you told M and Molly, in the bathroom," I inform her. "I came in right behind you guys but then left before you saw me. Bri, how could you?" Again, tears threaten, this time as much from anger as humiliation.

After a moment of hesitation, she frowns, her chagrin shifting to stubbornness. "Oh, come on, Deb, I did you a favor! Just like you've done for me, plenty of times. Remember last year, how you wheedled Matt into asking me to Homecoming? You nudged Gary my way, too, at the start of this year. I was just paying you back."

I want to tell her those were different, that she never cared as much about Matt or Gary as I do for Lucas. Except I'm not ready to admit how deeply I *do* care. Maybe not even to myself. So I just shrug again, instead.

"Besides," she continues, "it's not like Liam would have asked *me* if Kira hadn't put him up to it. For all we know, Lucas would've asked you anyway, because of what she said to them both. Maybe Liam was just a little quicker following through."

"Maybe," I grudgingly admit. "Still, I…wish you'd told me."

She regards me shrewdly. "Would you have enjoyed yourself as much tonight if I had?"

"That's not—" I begin hotly, then pause. "Okay, maybe not. I'd have felt like a charity case the whole dance, instead of just the last half hour. Like I do now. At least now I know why Lucas acted so… so *proper* all evening. He barely even touched me during the slow dances." My gut twists again with embarrassment at the memory.

"Yeah, well, Liam wasn't exactly forward, either," Bri admits, surprising me a little. "And not for lack of encouragement."

That makes me feel a *little* better. "You think they belong to some really strict religion or something? I mean, there's definitely *something* different about them. About all those new NuAgra folks, really." Like not knowing what "break the ice" meant.

Bri lifts a shoulder, grinning now. "If so, it just makes the new guys more of a challenge. Gorgeous as they all are, you can't say they're not worth the effort. Of course, Molly has Tristan all locked up now, and Trina was all *over* Alan tonight, the little slut. If you're right about them all being super religious, it's no wonder he looked so uncomfortable."

We both laugh and my earlier mortification fades. A little.

"Thanks, Bri. Sorry I snapped at you."

"No, I don't blame you. I feel really bad you heard me tell the others that—I should have just kept my big mouth shut. Still friends?" She opens her arms to me.

I step in and hug her. "Best friends," I affirm. "I'd better get home, though—it's late. And cold. G'night, Bri."

"Night, Deb."

She goes inside and I crunch through the thin layer of snow to my house next door, relieved we didn't end up in a real fight. Because Bri's not just my *best* friend, she's the only really close girlfriend I have these days. M seems to have totally adopted Molly as *her* new best friend, after spending all spring and summer in Ireland with the O'Gara family.

Sure, it gets old sometimes being referred to as Bri's "cute little friend," but she and I almost always have fun hanging out together. I'd really hate to lose that.

Especially since it's looking awfully unlikely now that I'll ever be *more* than friends with Lucas Walsh.

Order **_Unraveling the Stars_**, to keep reading!

A Note from Brenda Hiatt

I know there are a whole slew of holiday books out there to choose from, so I'd like to personally thank you for choosing and reading *Yuletide Perils!*

The idea for the *Starstruck series* grew in my mind over a period of years until I simply had to write it down to share with others. Since then, I've heard from many, many readers who seem to love these characters and their world every bit as much as I do, which makes me very happy. If you also enjoyed this book, please consider leaving a review wherever you buy or talk about books to let other like-minded readers know they might enjoy it, too.

Happy reading!
~Brenda :)

About the Author

Brenda writes novels of sparkling romantic adventure spanning Regency England, Americana, contemporary teen science fiction and more. Whichever you pick up, you'll find excitement, romance and, always, an uplifting happy ending. In addition to writing, Brenda is passionate about embracing life to the fullest, to include scuba diving (she has over 60 dives to her credit), Taekwondo (where she's currently working toward her 4th degree black belt), hiking, traveling…and reading, of course!

For a free Starstruck short story and the earliest news about Brenda Hiatt's books, subscribe to her newsletter at:
brendahiatt.com/subscribe

Connect with Brenda at:
brendahiatt.com